D0310356

THE BEAST OF BUCKINGHAM PALACE

Previously written by David Walliams:

THE BOY IN THE DRESS

MR STINK

BILLIONAIRE BOY

GANGSTA GRANNY

RATBURGER

DEMON DENTIST

AWFUL AUNTIE

GRANDPA'S GREAT ESCAPE

THE MIDNIGHT GANG

BAD DAD

THE ICE MONSTER

FING

THE WORLD'S WORST CHILDREN

THE WORLD'S WORST CHILDREN 2

THE WORLD'S WORST CHILDREN 3

THE WORLD'S WORST TEACHERS

Also available in picture book:

THE SLIGHTLY ANNOYING ELEPHANT

THE FIRST HIPPO ON THE MOON

THE QUEEN'S ORANG-UTAN

THE BEAR WHO WENT BOO!

THERE'S A SNAKE IN MY SCHOOL!

BOOGIE BEAR

GERONIMO

David Walliams

THE BEAST OF BUCKINGHAM PALACE

Illustrated by Tony Ross

HarperCollins *Children's Books*

First published in Great Britain by
HarperCollins *Children's Books* in 2019
HarperCollins *Children's Books* is a division of HarperCollins*Publishers* Ltd,
HarperCollins Publishers
1 London Bridge Street
London SE1 9GF

The HarperCollins website address is:
www.harpercollins.co.uk

1

HB ISBN 978–0–00–826217–4
TPB ISBN 978–0–00–838564–4
PB ISBN 978–0–00–838965–9

A CIP catalogue record for this title is available from the British Library.

Printed and bound in England by CPI Group (UK) Ltd, Croydon CR0 4YY

MIX
Paper from
responsible sources
FSC™ C007454

This book is produced from independently certified FSC™ paper
to ensure responsible forest management.

For more information visit: www.harpercollins.co.uk/green

For my brave friend Henry.

David x

THANK-YOUS

I WOULD LIKE TO THANK

ANN-JANINE MURTAGH
My Executive Publisher

CHARLIE REDMAYNE
CEO

TONY ROSS
My Illustrator

PAUL STEVENS
My Literary Agent

HARRIET WILSON
My Editor

KATE BURNS
Art Editor

SAMANTHA STEWART
Managing Editor

GERALDINE STROUD
My PR Director

VAL BRATHWAITE
Creative Director

DAVID McDOUGALL
Art Director

ELORINE GRANT
Deputy Art Director

KATE CLARKE
Designer

MATTHEW KELLY
Designer

TANYA HOUGHAM
My Audio Editor

David Walliams

One hundred years

in the future.

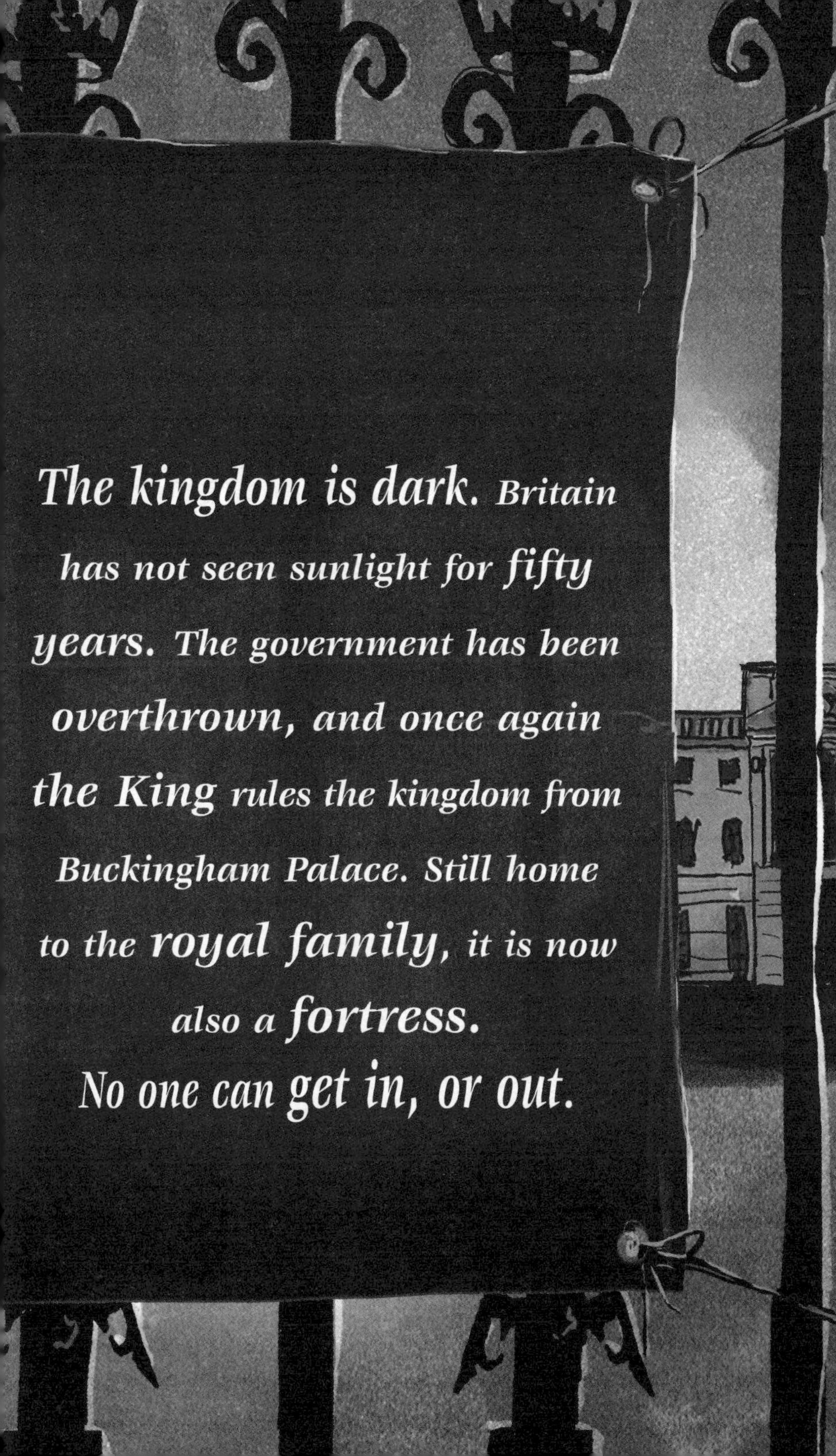
The kingdom is dark. Britain
has not seen sunlight for fifty
years. The government has been
overthrown, and once again
the King rules the kingdom from
Buckingham Palace. Still home
to the royal family, it is now
also a fortress.
No one can get in, or out.

These are the characters in the story…

PRINCE ALFRED *is a sickly boy of twelve, who has never known life outside Buckingham Palace.*

THE KING *was once a great ruler and a kind father. Now he is as lost as his kingdom.*

THE QUEEN *is an impossibly posh lady, who is much loved by her son. She and Alfred have an unbreakable bond.*

THE LORD PROTECTOR *is a learned man who began his royal career forty years ago in the palace library. He has risen to become the King's closest adviser, but yearns for more power.*

MITE *is a homeless orphan from the outside. She is so called because of her small size. Her parents were killed when she was a toddler, and since then she has had to fend for herself.*

NANNY *is a lady in her eighties who in her job has looked after two generations of royal children. She cared for the King when he was a boy and is now the nanny to Prince Alfred.*

THE OLD QUEEN *is an elderly lady who was Queen when her husband was King. Now she is deemed to be a traitor, and is living somewhere in exile, though no one knows where. Except her, of course.*

LADY AGATHA *and* LADY ENID *are two of the Old Queen's ladies-in-waiting. As ladies-in-waiting, they performed various duties for the Old Queen, such as tending to her dresses, carrying bouquets of flowers and typing letters. Now they too live in exile with four other ladies-in-waiting: Lady Beatrix, Lady Virginia, Lady Daphne and Lady Judith.*

BEATRIX

DAPHNE

VIRGINIA

THE ROYAL GUARDS *are elite soldiers in gold skull masks and flowing red robes. They are armed with laser guns, and their mission is to protect the palace at all costs.*

THE EXECUTIONER *is a giant of a man whose face is covered by a black hood. He is in charge of all the torture and executions at the Tower of London.*

THE OCTOBUT *is an eight-armed robot that is meant to perform the same tasks as a human butler.*

THE ALL-SEEING EYE *is a flying robot that resembles a giant eye. It is under the control of the Lord Protector, so he can monitor everyone and everything in Buckingham Palace.*

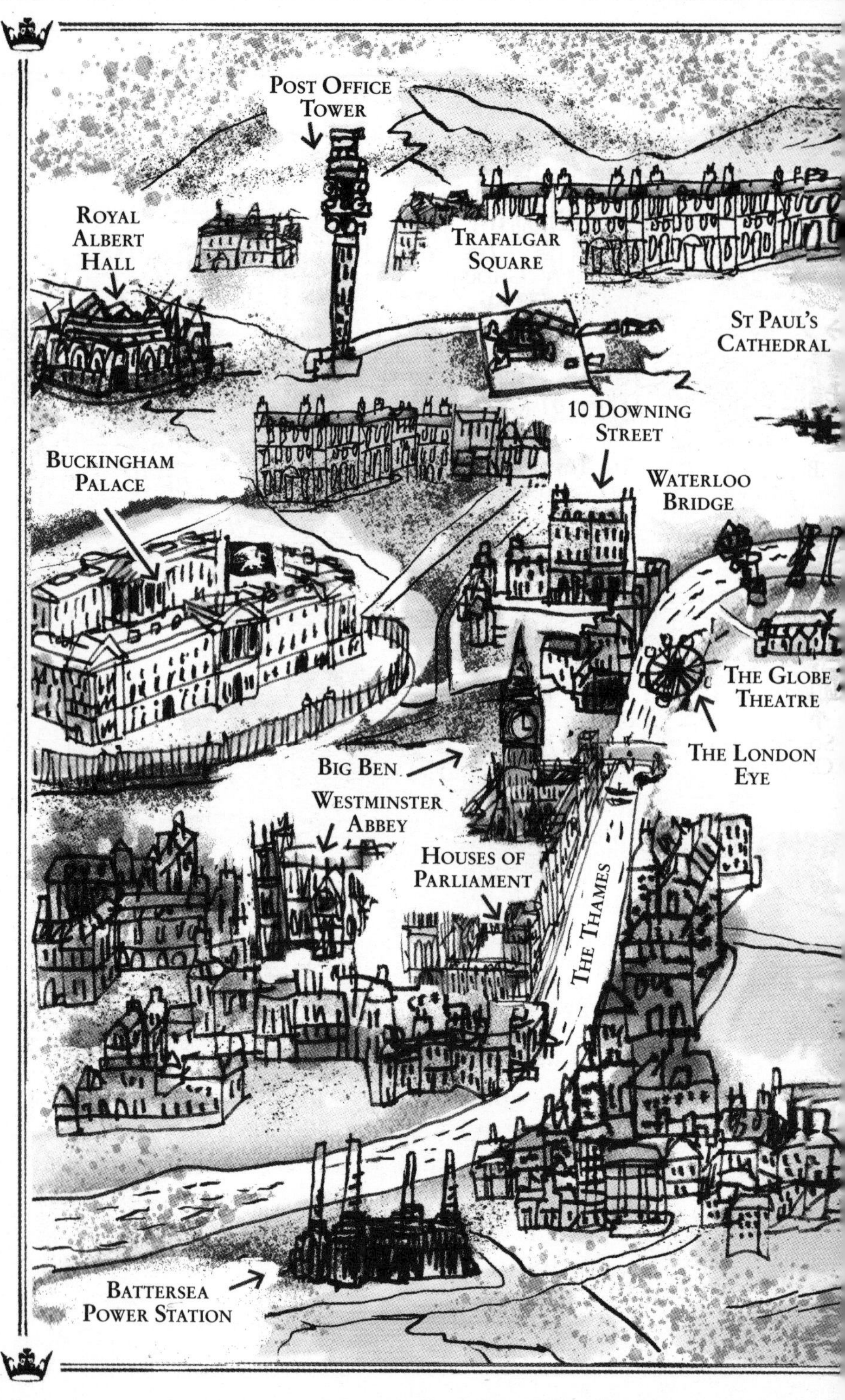
Post Office Tower
Royal Albert Hall
Trafalgar Square
St Paul's Cathedral
10 Downing Street
Buckingham Palace
Waterloo Bridge
The Globe Theatre
The London Eye
Big Ben
Westminster Abbey
Houses of Parliament
The Thames
Battersea Power Station

THE GHERKIN
BLACKFRIARS BRIDGE
THE TOWER OF LONDON
TOWER BRIDGE
HMS *BELFAST*
SOUTHWARK CATHEDRAL
THE SHARD
STATUE OF DAVID WALLIAMS
LONDON
c.2120

Inside **BUCKINGHAM PALACE** c. 2120

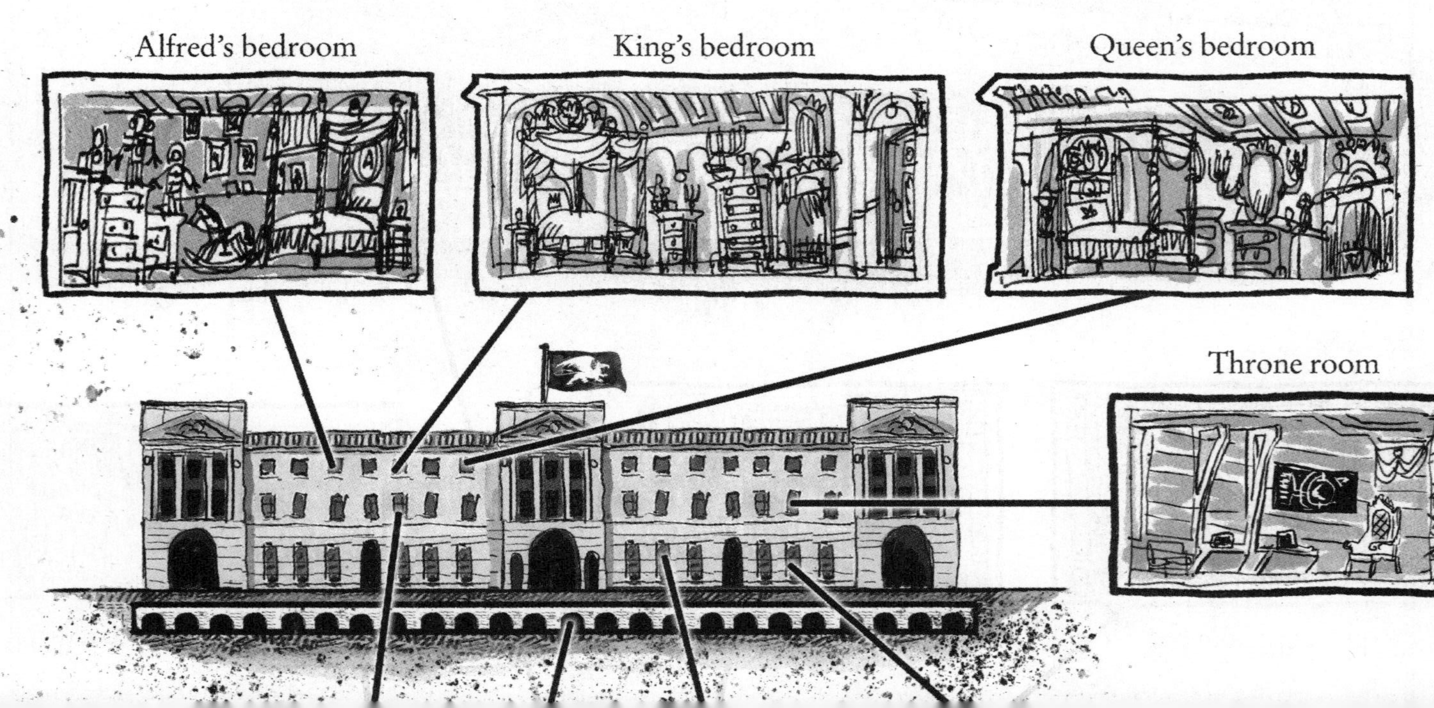

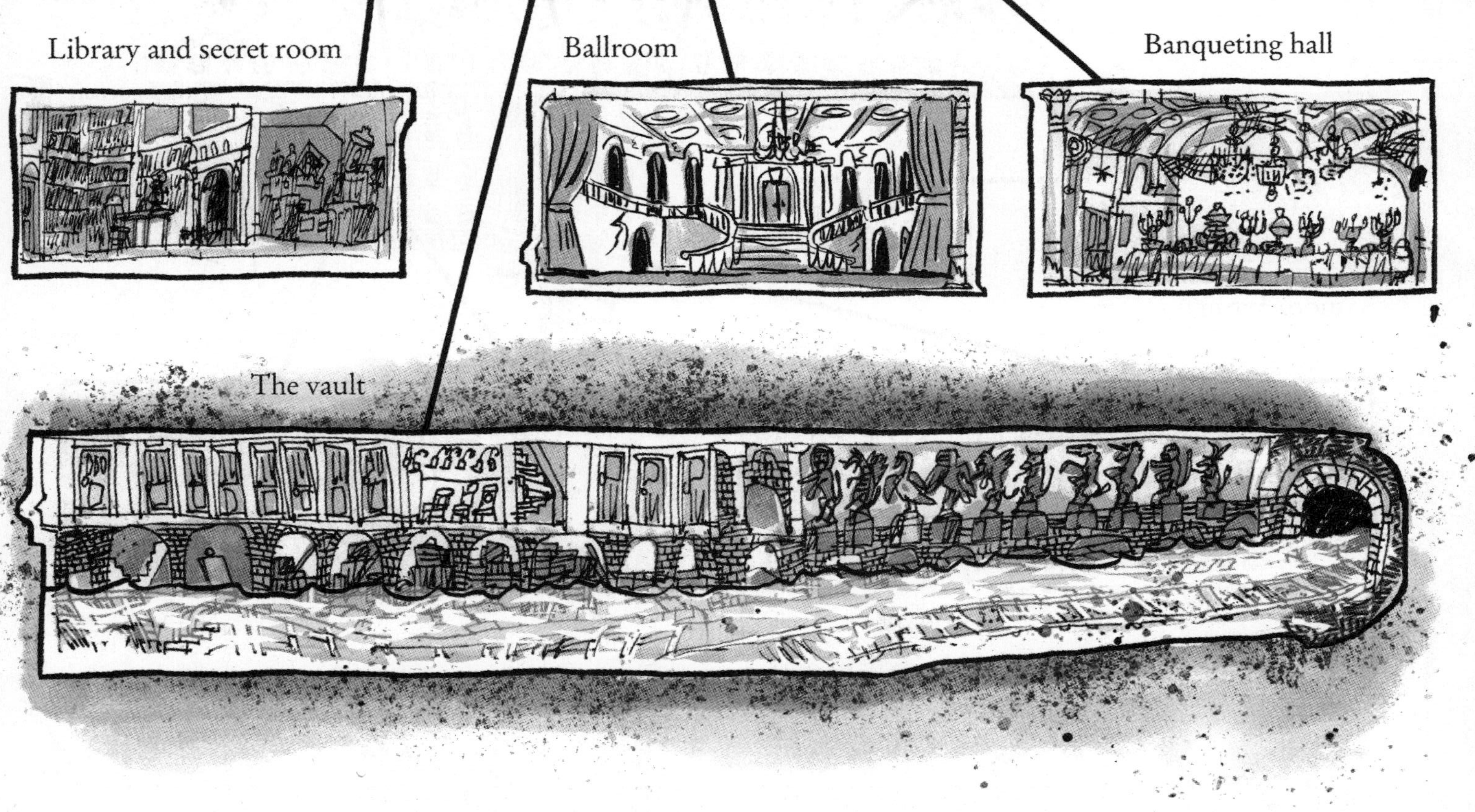
Library and secret room
Ballroom
Banqueting hall
The vault

Prologue

The griffin is the King of the Beasts. It is half eagle (the King of the Birds) and half lion (the King of the Animals). The head and wings are those of an eagle, while the body and back legs are those of a lion.

For centuries, the beast has been thought of as the stuff of legend.

Early civilisations worshipped the griffin – it can be found in stories from both Ancient Egypt and Ancient Greece.

In medieval times, this half eagle, half lion became a symbol of godlike power.

The power over life and death.

The power to create or destroy the universe.

Infinite power for all eternity.

The sight of a griffin would inspire terror in the hearts of all men. That is why the beasts were used as symbols through the centuries by kings and queens. Griffins can be seen on coats of arms, flags and shields. The message was simple: **kneel or you will suffer a terrible fate at the claws of this beast.**

It looks a little like a dinosaur, those terrifying creatures that stalked the Earth millions of years ago. However, unlike dinosaurs, no one has ever found the skeleton of one.

But that doesn't mean that a griffin never lived.

Or one day might not live again...

PART ONE

The Coming of the Beast

CHAPTER 1

Dark

It was noon, and the sky was black.

There had been darkness over the kingdom for half a century. For, many years before, the people of the Earth had not taken care of their home.

They had **burned** down all the forests, reducing every last tree to ash.

They had **pumped** the rivers, lakes and seas full of waste, killing all the fish.

They had dug **deeper** and **deeper** under the ground for oil, until the planet was hollow to its core.

Eventually, the Earth took its **revenge**.

The ice caps of the Arctic and the Antarctic **melted**. The floods were so mighty that whole countries became **submerged** underwater.

Violent earthquakes **shook** entire cities to the ground. All that was left behind were **piles and piles of rubble.**

Volcanoes **erupted**, pumping billions of tonnes of ash into the air. Without the sunlight, the crops **withered and died**. Nothing could grow.

The kingdom was plunged into an **ETERNAL WINTER**.

It was the only world Alfred knew. He was already twelve years old, but had never, ever seen sunlight. Often, he dreamed how it must have been to feel the sun on your face, or run through a field of tall grass, or swim in a sunlit sea. But it was just that, a dream.

The boy had seen pictures of the sun in books and marvelled at it. A perfect circle of gold. Now the moon and stars had become invisible too. Alfred would spend hours and hours imagining how the night sky must have looked with a thousand little lights twinkling through the blackness.

He was one of those children who liked nothing more than being alone with his imagination. In truth, he had little choice, having been sickly his whole life. Soon after he was born, he became ill. As a baby, Alfred had not been expected to survive, but survive he did.

Just.

The child was as pale as snow and as thin as dust. He wore thick glasses to aid his poor eyesight. Often Alfred was so weak he had to stay in bed all day. Thank goodness all around his bed were piles and piles of books. Books, books and more books. Books about animals. Books about space. Books about trees. Books about dinosaurs. Books about books.

Books about history were his absolute favourite.

The trouble was that there was a strict curfew in the building where Alfred lived. Night was the most dangerous time. That was when there was most chance of an attack from the outside. Lights had to be out at eight o'clock sharp. By order of the King. Anyone caught with lights on would be severely punished. Punishments were brutal in the kingdom. Those in power had returned to medieval forms of torture.

The Rack

The Scold's Bridle

The Rats' Dungeon

The Head-crusher

The Iron Chair

Despite the strict rules, the boy loved his books so much that he would carry on reading by candlelight under his bedcovers…

The night our story begins, Alfred was doing just that. He was reading a weighty leather-bound book about the kings and queens of Britain through the ages. The first known one was **Alfred the Great**. He had become ruler an impossibly long time ago, in **871**. The boy was named after that first king, but it was hard to believe anybody would ever describe this Alfred as "great". He felt anything but.

As the boy was devouring the story of the beheading of King Charles I in 1649, a deafening sound rocked the room.

KABOOM!

Alfred dropped his book.

THUD!

And his candle. He very nearly set the covers alight.

WOOF!

Smothering the flames and blowing the candle out…

WHOOSH!

…he pulled off his bedcovers.

WHIP!

A huge explosion outside had illuminated the boy's bedroom with glowing red, orange and yellow light.

Alfred slid out of bed and using all his strength limped over to his huge bay window. Just those few steps left him painfully out of breath.

"Huh! Huh! Huh!"

He leaned on the window frame to steady himself.

Alfred's bedroom was high up on the top floor. From here, he could see far across London. A building was ablaze. But not just any building.

St Paul's Cathedral.

This historic structure, perhaps one of the most famous in the world, had been destroyed.

Its huge white dome cracked as if it were nothing more than an egg. Huge plumes of black smoke billowed high into the air.

Oh no! thought Alfred. *No! Not St Paul's!*

He had seen many London landmarks destroyed over the years. Nelson's Column had been toppled to the ground.

CRUNCH!

The London Eye had plunged into the River Thames.

SPLASH!

The Royal Albert Hall roof had caved in after a bomb had blasted it to pieces.

BOOM!

However, none of these was as sacred as St Paul's. This was a new low. The cathedral had been built after the Great Fire of London in 1666. The glorious structure had miraculously survived the Blitz, when Nazi bombs rained down on London during World War Two, but now it was burning to the ground.

Alfred's next thought was, ***Revolutionaries***.

This had all the hallmarks of one of their attacks.

The boy had never met anyone from this top-secret organisation, but the Lord Protector had taught him much about them. From what Alfred had been told, the **revolutionaries** hated the fact that power had returned to the King. They wanted to overthrow him, and behead him, just like the Roundheads had done to Charles I during the English Civil War.

These **revolutionaries** stood only for death and destruction. That is why the Lord Protector said they needed to be crushed at all costs.

RAT! TAT! TAT!

There was a burst of machine-gun fire.

"NOOO!"

The distant sound of shouts.

"ARGH!"

Was that a scream?

Alfred shivered. As much as he wanted to look away, he couldn't. Every day there were attacks all over London, but explosions on this scale were rare. The boy pressed his hand up against the cold, thick glass and looked out at the devastation.

This was the kingdom Alfred would one day inherit.

CHAPTER 2

Lionheart

Alfred was as far from an ordinary twelve-year-old boy as you could imagine. Inside he felt ordinary, but he'd been told time and time again by grown-ups that he was anything but.

Alfred was not just plain old "Alfred".

He was "Prince Alfred".

His father was the King.

One day he himself would be crowned King.

King Alfred II, ruler of Britain and all its people.

The strange thing was that he would become king of a kingdom he had never set foot in. Not once had he been outside Buckingham Palace.

The boy's sad face could often be glimpsed at his bedroom window at the very top of the building. Just above his window, a flag flew on the roof of the palace. For hundreds of years it had been the Union Jack, the red, white and blue flag of the United Kingdom. Now a very different flag flew, one that the Lord Protector himself had instigated. It was a black flag, with a golden griffin at its centre. This was the symbol of the new order of things. Britain now had no government, so no prime minister or politicians representing the people. It also had no police force. Instead, the King's personal army, the royal guards, enforced the rule of law.

Buckingham Palace had been home to the British royal family for centuries, since the time of George III. From his history books, Alfred had learned that it had become a royal residence way back in 1761.

The palace used to be a sanctuary.

Now it was a fortress.

Members of the royal guard were stationed all along the perimeter wall. The soldiers were instantly recognisable by their long flowing red robes, hoods and horrifying gold skull masks. On their arms they wore black bands, with the golden griffin at the centre, just like on the flag. Despite looking almost medieval, the royal guards were armed with laser guns. Just one zap was enough to blast someone into oblivion. These soldiers guarded those who lived inside Buckingham Palace.

The palace had seen better days. The carpets were worn and the wallpaper was peeling off the walls, but it was still a special place. The prince's bedroom was furnished only with antiques. He slept on a four-poster bed in silk pyjamas, though the bed creaked and the pyjamas had holes in them.

The palace kitchen was stocked with every dish imaginable, as long as it came out of a tin. There were food stocks to last a hundred years or more.

Alfred was safe inside the palace. Or so he thought.

The boy pressed his face closer to the window as the domed roof of St Paul's Cathedral caved in. Despite the horror, Alfred couldn't look away. Then, in an instant, he became distracted. There was a commotion in the corridor. He could hear a struggle and shouts just beyond his bedroom door.

"TAKE YOUR FILTHY HANDS OFF ME! HOW DARE YOU! I AM YOUR QUEEN!"

It was his mother's voice.

As fast as he could, which wasn't very fast, Alfred limped across his bedroom, and opened the door. The Queen was being held roughly by two members of the royal guard. They were meant to protect the royal family, so why were they dragging her along as if she were a criminal?

These were strange times, but this was the strangest time of all.

"MAMA!" cried Alfred after her.

The Queen was wearing her long lace nightdress and one slipper. Even though she was being manhandled, she was trying to maintain some sense of dignity. This was a lady who prided herself on never having a hair out of place.

Alfred had not seen his mother without her hair perfectly lacquered in a "do" and her face painted with make-up. Right now, her do was unravelling fast.

Instead of make-up her face was covered with thick night cream. She looked a sight. Alfred idolised his mother, and it was weird seeing her like this.

"ALFRED!" she shouted over her shoulder, struggling with the soldiers to make them stop.

Because their faces were hidden behind gold skull masks, it was impossible to guess what they were thinking. The royal guards remained silent throughout, which only added to the sense that this was a **nightmare.**

"Mama! Where are they taking you?" demanded Alfred.

"GET BACK INSIDE YOUR ROOM, ALFRED! AND LOCK THE DOOR!"

she shouted back.

"But…!"

"NOW! AND PROMISE ME YOU'LL STAY THERE!"

The boy did not reply.

"Promise!" she pleaded.

"I promise!" he mumbled.

Shocked at what he'd just witnessed, Alfred retreated and slammed his bedroom door shut.

SCHTUM!

He stood dead still, unable to move. It was as if he were underwater. That too made it feel like being in a nightmare.

But this was no nightmare. This was really happening.

As if to prove that, tears welled in the boy's eyes, then streamed down his face. His mother, who he loved more than anyone, was being dragged away in the night, and he was helpless to stop it. Alfred looked around his bedroom. There were silver-framed photographs of her everywhere.

Here she was reading him a bedtime story.

There she was pushing him on a rocking horse.

Here she was helping him draw a picture.

There she was playing with his train set.

Here she was painting his face like a lion.

There she was helping him blow out all the candles on a birthday cake.

Here she was giving him a teddy bear.

In each picture, the young boy was basking in the glow of her love.

In one of the photographs, Alfred was dressed up in a suit of armour as Richard the Lionheart. Richard I was a heroic king from the twelfth century, who led crusades in far-off lands. Alfred picked up the picture, and studied it.

Lionheart.

That was his mother's pet name for him.

Tears welled in the boy's eyes. He always felt unworthy of that name. He felt nothing like a hero.

Having been ill all his life, Alfred was used to being an object of pity. Sometimes he even pitied himself.

Tears ran down his cheeks.

He felt helpless to stop his mother being dragged away by the royal guards.

Other important people had mysteriously disappeared in the night over the years.

The prime minister.

The chief of police.

The head of the army.

Even Alfred's grandmother had suffered the same fate.

Lionheart.

His mother's voice calling him that name circled round and round in his mind.

Lionheart.

Lionheart had been a mighty warrior. Alfred needed to summon some of his great-great-great-great-great-great-great-great-great-great-great-great-great-great-great-great-great-great-great-ancestor's spirit, and do something. Anything.

"Lionheart!" he said out loud, and, despite what he had promised his mother, he opened his bedroom door.

C

R

E

A

K!

CHAPTER 3

Faceless Fiends

Alfred limped down the corridor, steadying himself on the sideboard to catch his breath. Quite a few paces ahead, the royal guards' cloaks fluttered as they bustled the boy's mother along. Alfred tried to speed up, but in doing so he stumbled over a rug…

THOD!

…twisting his ankle.

"OUCH!"

With no chance of catching up with them, he thought of Richard the Lionheart, and called out, "I C-C-COMMAND YOU TO ST-ST-STOP!"

Not only was Alfred out of breath, but he was not used to giving orders. As a result, the words came out wonky. Despite Alfred being royal and these being the royal guards, the pair of faceless fiends ignored him. The Queen turned her head and shouted back to her son.

"PLEASE, ALFRED! I DON'T WANT YOU TO SEE THIS."

There was a look of terror in her eyes. A look the boy had never seen before. His mother had always been a wonder at pretending everything was tickety-boo when it clearly wasn't. She would always make up stories to cover what was really going on.

The sound of an explosion in the middle of the night was "nothing more than a thunderstorm". She would then stroke Alfred's head until he drifted off back to sleep.

After his grandmother had mysteriously gone

missing one night from the palace, Mother would make believe that Grammy had written postcards to him. She was the "Old Queen", his father's widowed mother, and much loved by the boy. Alfred always called her "Grammy" because when he was little he couldn't say "Granny". His mother would read these postcards aloud to him as she put him to bed at night.

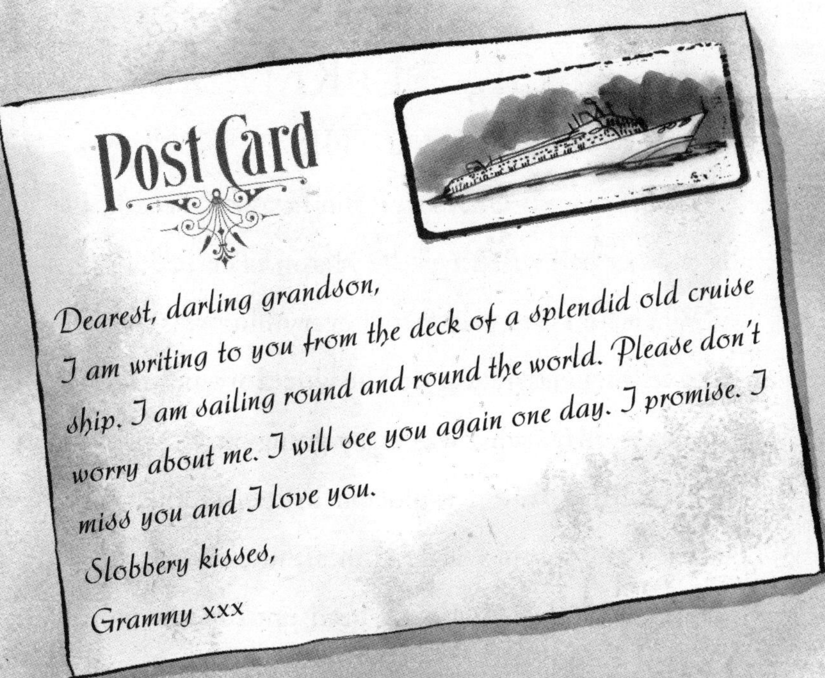
Post Card

Dearest, darling grandson,
I am writing to you from the deck of a splendid old cruise ship. I am sailing round and round the world. Please don't worry about me. I will see you again one day. I promise. I miss you and I love you.
Slobbery kisses,
Grammy xxx

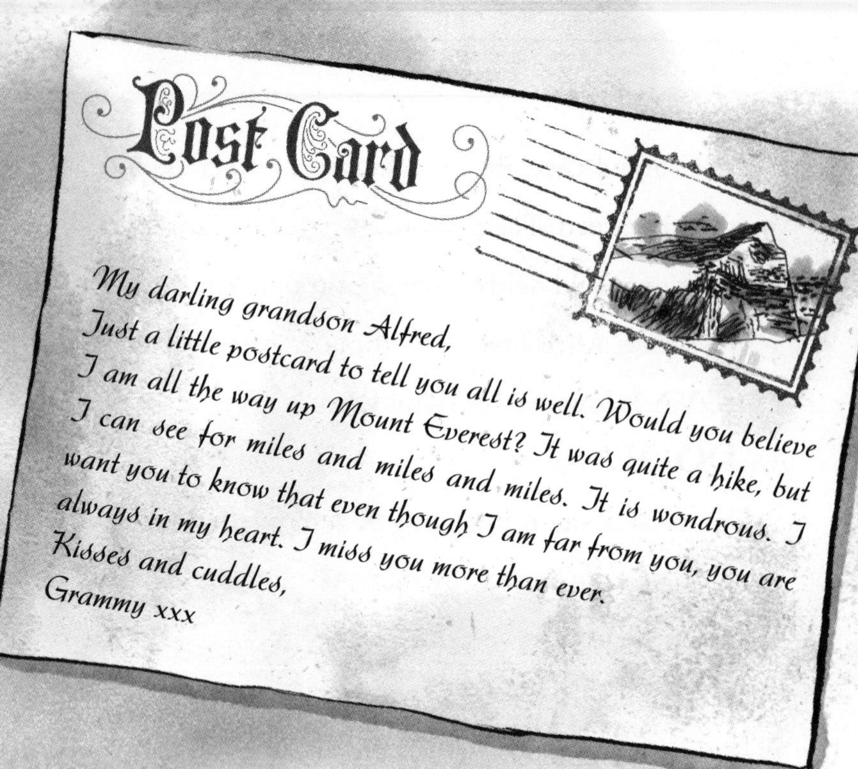

Post Card

My darling grandson Alfred,
Just a little postcard to tell you all is well. Would you believe
I am all the way up Mount Everest? It was quite a hike, but
I can see for miles and miles and miles. It is wondrous. I
want you to know that even though I am far from you, you are
always in my heart. I miss you more than ever.
Kisses and cuddles,
Grammy xxx

It was only when Alfred grew older that he suspected his mother had written all the postcards herself.

When he asked whether they would ever set foot outside Buckingham Palace, the Queen would take her son on an imaginary flight around the world.

"Hold my hand and together let's fly up, up, up into the air, across London, across the sea, over the pyramids of Egypt, down the Grand Canyon of America, along the Great Wall of China and back to Dear Old Blighty in time for tea."

In his mind's eye, the boy would see everything his mother described. The adventures gave him hope that one day he would be able to leave the palace.

Just then Alfred felt something – or someone – SLAM down on his shoulders.

DOOF!

He took a sharp intake of breath, but he was so shocked that no sound came out of his mouth. Two large gloved hands were holding on to him. Alfred turned round. It was another royal guard who had somehow crept up on the boy after he'd stumbled on the rug. Silent, just like the others, he picked the prince up with ease and dragged him back to his bedroom.

"L-L-LET ME GO! I SAID, L-L-LET ME G-G-GO!"

Alfred was powerless to resist. In moments, he was deposited back in his bedroom, and the door shut behind him.

SHTUM!

He lingered behind the door and listened. Outside, the guard waited for a while before the sound of footsteps betrayed his movements. In his head Alfred counted to a hundred. As much as he wanted to race through the numbers, he knew that was a foolish idea. He needed to count until he thought the coast would be clear.

"Ninety-seven, ninety-eight, ninety-nine, one hundred."

On one hundred, he opened his bedroom door slowly and silently. Then he peeped out and checked that no one was around. The corridor was clear. So he tiptoed down it, before hurrying down the long, sweeping staircase, and across to the grand ballroom. This room once played host to the world's most extravagant parties. Now it was a ghost of a room. The chandelier was hanging by a thread, the silk curtains drooped on the floor and damp had blotted the walls with dark, ugly patches. Desperately out of breath, the sickly boy stumbled again. This time he fell flat on his face.

BANG!

"OOF!"

Alfred noticed there was some kind of powder on his hands and face. At first, he thought it was dust – the palace was encrusted with the stuff. But it wasn't dust. This had a smell to it that was different.

Chalk!

Scrambling to his feet, he noticed that there were faint chalk markings all across the vast floor. It was as if the boy were standing at the centre of a life-sized chessboard. Someone had tried to rub the lines and markings off, but traces were left behind. Alfred bent down. There were words and symbols, but, despite his love of books, he couldn't recognise any of them. What's more, there were burn marks on the wood, and a large discoloured area where something heavy had been moved.

Alfred shivered as he realised something: there were strange goings-on in the palace.

The boy stood up and walked slap bang into someone.

D
O
O
F!

Or, rather, not someone, but something.

THE OCTOBUT.

A robot programmed to do all a butler's duties, it was meant to make life easier, but it actually made it harder. Much harder. It looked not unlike an octopus, if an octopus were made of metal and trundled across the ground. Crucially, though, it did have eight arms, each one with a special attachment for performing different tasks. Hence the name: "Octo" for "octopus", and "but" for "butler", although its name made it sound more like it was an octopus's bottom.

THE OCTOBUT had the following arm attachments:

"Good morning, Mr President!" jabbered the OCTOBUT. It was always getting things wrong.

"Oh, hello, OCTOBUT," whispered Alfred. "I wasn't expecting to bump into you. Please can you keep your voice down?"

"Roast chicken," replied the robot, before announcing, "You will be pleased to know I have boil-washed your underpants."

With that, the OCTOBUT flung a gigantic pair of unwashed men's underpants at the prince. They must have belonged to some humongous old man.

WHOOSH!

They landed SLAP BANG in the boy's face.

"Thank you, OCTOBUT," whispered Alfred as he removed the still-stinky underpants from his nose.

"Now, are you ready for your game of croquet?"

"No!" hissed the boy.

The robot swung its croquet-mallet arm so hard it bashed the wall.

BANG!

So hard that the arm itself came loose.

It fell to the floor with a CRASH.

With seven arms rather than eight, it was now not so much an OCTOBUT as a Septemabut.*

Outside the ballroom, Alfred could hear the bootsteps of royal guards growing nearer.

STOMP! STOMP! STOMP!

The soldiers were just outside the tall wooden double doors that led into the ballroom.

"You go that way!" urged the boy, spinning the OCTOBUT round to face in their direction. "The pope needs his toenails clipping."

"Very good, Princess!" came the reply.

---

* "*Septem*" is the Latin word for "seven".

With all his might, Alfred pushed the OCTOBUT so it trundled off in the direction of the doors.

As the boy tiptoed out of the ballroom, he looked back to see the OCTOBUT CRASH straight into the guards, knocking them to the floor, and accidentally slapping one in the face with its corgi-stroking hand.

SLAP!

SLAP!

SLAP!

The guard grabbed the arm to make the robot stop, and it came off in his hands.

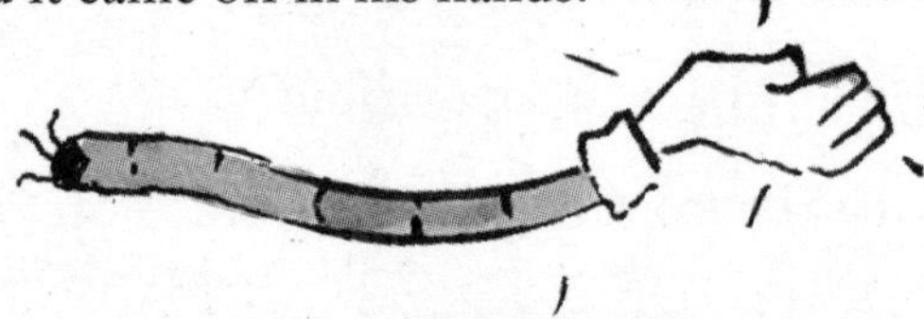

"Oh no!" exclaimed the robot. "I will never stroke a corgi again!"

The poor OCTOBUT was now down to six arms. It should really be renamed the Sexabut but that sounds far too rude.

Ahead of Alfred was the entrance to the throne room.

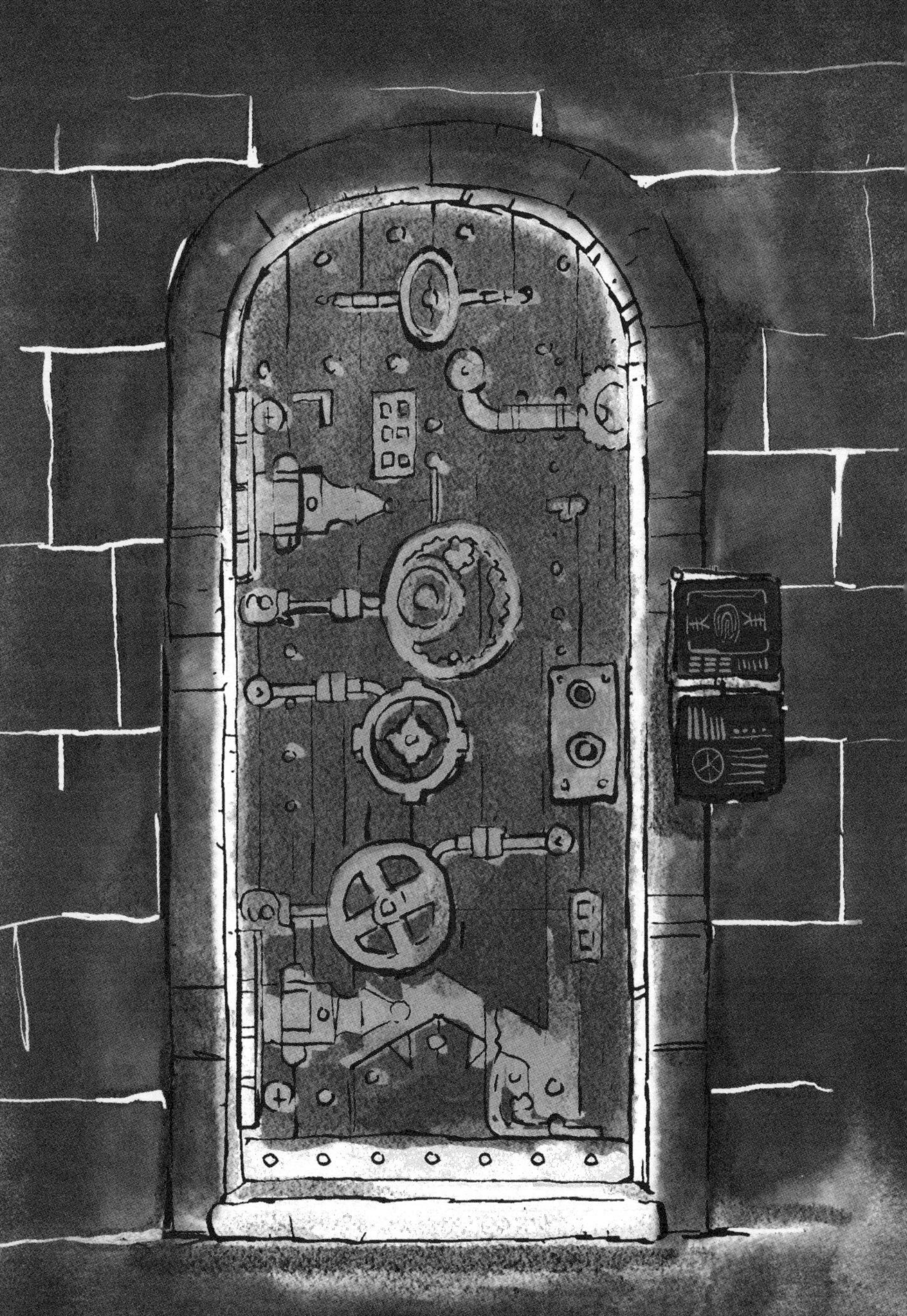

This was the fortress within the fortress of Buckingham Palace. In a way, it was a panic room, like a giant safe. It had been installed in case of an attack, or, horror upon horror, in case the **revolutionaries** ever managed to break into the palace itself. The walls of the throne room had been made of metre-thick steel. The only way in or out was through a huge metal door, which opened only with fingerprint recognition. Just two people had access to that room.

The first was the boy's father, the King.

The second was the King's chief adviser, the Lord Protector.

The Lord Protector was an elegant figure in his sixties. He was well-spoken and refined, with impeccable manners. A learned man, he spoke with great authority on any subject you might care to mention. Art. Literature. Philosophy. He wore a black shirt buttoned up to the top without a tie, and a smart grey suit. On his lapel he sported a gold pin badge, which, like the flag and the armbands the royal guards wore, depicted a griffin.

The Lord Protector had worked at Buckingham Palace for as long as anyone could remember. He'd started off in the palace library, tending to the thousands of ancient books collected there.

Most of the books were displayed on shelves, but there was a handful kept under lock and key in a cabinet. Only the Lord Protector had the key. Like museum pieces, Alfred was not allowed to take these books up to his room. However, he could look at their covers. One intrigued him the most. It was an ancient red leather-bound book with gold lettering on the front.

The boy knew very little Latin, but he knew enough to translate that. "*Libro*" was a word you often found in library books. It meant "book".

So this was ***The Book of Albion***.

Once, when he'd slipped into the library unnoticed, Alfred had seen the Lord Protector studying it. Glancing over the man's shoulder, he saw there were ornate hand-painted pictures inside. But, before he could make out what they were, the Lord Protector had slammed the book shut, and locked it back in the case. Of course, this only intrigued the boy more.

Over the years, the Lord Protector had gained the trust of the King to the extent that he had become his closest adviser.

As the country slid into ruin with crops failing and no clean water to drink, the Lord Protector introduced **EXTREME MEASURES** in the King's name.

- Food and water were rationed.
- There were curfews at night, so people couldn't go outside.
- Punishments were severe, including execution.
- The government was outlawed.
- The army and the police force were disbanded and replaced by the royal guard.
- The Union Jack was replaced by the flag of the griffin.

Since the catastrophic events that had plunged the kingdom into darkness, the King had relied heavily on the Lord Protector to guide him through this terrifying new world. Over the years, the King became more and more withdrawn, as if he'd disappeared into the back of his mind. No one knew why exactly, but the King, who had once been so full of life, seemed as if he were one of the walking dead. Soon he was ruler only in name. The country was controlled by the Lord Protector.

When Alfred spied his mother being held by the royal guards outside the huge metal door to the throne room, he seized his chance. The lady was making a lot of noise, and struggling to get away, which distracted the two soldiers.

"THIS IS NO WAY TO TREAT YOUR QUEEN! UNHAND ME! DO YOU HEAR? UNHAND ME AT ONCE!"

The boy tiptoed behind them, and when the metal door slid open…

WHOOSH!

...he took a deep

breath,

and

sneaked in.

CHAPTER 4

A Lost Soul

The throne room was modern and high-tech compared to the rest of Buckingham Palace, which had not changed for centuries. The walls, floor and ceiling were silver metal. One side was covered with a giant television screen, affording any view of the palace imaginable from a roving flying robot.

In front of the screen was a figure, slumped on the throne.

The King.

The man was only in his fifties, but he looked a good deal older. He had a long, grey beard, and deep, dark circles round his eyes. His appearance had changed rapidly over the years. This once-handsome upright man, full of *life* and *love* and *laughter*, had become an empty shell. Alfred thought that something must have happened to him, something terrible, to make him like this. Father was a completely different man from how he'd been when Alfred was a toddler. It was disturbing to witness such a change in him. As always, the King was wearing his silk pyjamas and dressing gown. He never got dressed or shaved or even washed.

You would never guess he was the King. Once he'd been a great guardian of the British people – now he was seen as their enemy.

Behind the King stood the Lord Protector, his long, thin fingers creeping on to the back of the throne.

"Lord Protector! What in the name of Great Britain do you think you are doing?" demanded the Queen.

The Lord Protector looked past her and the two royal guards – he'd spotted the prince crouching behind them.

"Well, well, well. We have an uninvited guest," he purred.

"WHAT?" demanded the Queen. She looked round to see her son lurking there.

"I'm sorry, Mama."

The Queen was furious. "Alfred! I told you to stay in your room!"

"I know, but I couldn't just let them take you away. Not without a fight."

The Queen mouthed "I love you" to her son.

The boy mouthed "I love you too" back.

"FATHER!" shouted Alfred. "They are taking Mama away! You have to stop them!"

The King turned to his son, but his eyes had an absence about them, as if there were a deep sadness that no one could reach.

He was staring at Alfred, but seemed to look right through him into space. There appeared to be no thought or feeling within him.

"Your Royal Highness," began the Lord Protector, "with respect, this is neither the time nor the place for one of such tender years. Please let me call your nanny. She can escort you safely back to your room."

"NO!" snapped the boy, finding a strength he didn't know he had.

"No?" The Lord Protector had a way of being perfectly unruffled.

"NO! I demand to know what you are doing with my mother!"

The Queen allowed herself a smile, as if to say, "That's my boy!"

"Father! Please help us!"

The King held up his hand as if to say, "Enough." At once, his son noticed nasty cuts on the palm of his father's hand. He'd seen these before, although, when asked, his father had no memory whatsoever of how they'd got there.

The Lord Protector smirked. He spoke softly and slowly, not meeting the boy's anger.

"There must be some misunderstanding, Your Royal Highness. I am not doing anything to your mother, the Queen. I am merely a servant of the King."

The Queen glanced sadly at the King. "My husband is a lost soul and has been for many years, thanks to you. No, this is your doing, Lord Protector!" she stated. "What a title you have! *Protector!* You protect nothing and nobody other than yourself. You are destroying this kingdom, but you are not going to destroy me!"

The Lord Protector smiled and sighed. "Please forgive me, Your Majesty, but you are quite wrong. This is not my doing. Your arrest is a direct order from your husband, the King."

Neither the Queen nor the prince could believe what they were hearing.

"Father," called out the boy.

But the man did not respond.

"FATHER!"

The King's black eyes came to some semblance of life and fixed on his son.

"Alfred?" he asked. "Is that you?"

"Yes, Father. It's me, your son, Alfred!"

It had been days since he'd seen his father, and he seemed more distant than ever. "What are you doing, Father? Mother is being taken away by the guards. And the Lord Protector says it is on your direct order!"

The King gathered his thoughts and began. He spoke slowly and softly. "The **revolutionaries** struck again tonight. St Paul's Cathedral has been destroyed."

"A place of worship," sighed the Lord Protector. "Cruel and callous even by the standards of the revolutionary scum."

"What on earth has that got to do with me?" demanded the Queen.

The Lord Protector's mouth twitched into a ghoulish grin, but he said nothing.

The King continued, refusing to look his wife in the eye. "It has everything to do with you."

"This is nonsense!" she protested. "UTTER NONSENSE!"

The King's eyes flickered again, and he turned away. He couldn't bear to look at his wife as he spoke. "For some time, I am sorry to say, you have been under suspicion."

"Me?" she demanded. The lady was incredulous. "But I am the Queen!"

"You have been spied upon. And the All-Seeing Eye sees everything," added the Lord Protector.

"Intelligence information has been brought to my attention," continued the King, still unable to look at her, "that points to you being in direct communication with the **revolutionaries**."

The Queen glowed red and began spluttering her innocence. "But... I..."

"You don't deny it, Your Majesty?" pressed the Lord Protector.

"No, I, er..." the lady stuttered. "Of course, I deny it!"

"Then," began the Lord Protector, "why did you have this hidden in your bedroom?"

He lifted a cloth to reveal an old-fashioned radio crouched guiltily on a metal table. It had a microphone, a speaker and an aerial, and looked as if it dated back nearly two hundred years to World War Two.

"I have never seen that before in my life!" protested the Queen.

"It was found hidden in a secret compartment in your dressing room."

The radio crackled into life. A muffled voice on the other end said,

"THIS IS SCEPTRE CALLING REGINA – OVER. DO YOU READ ME?"

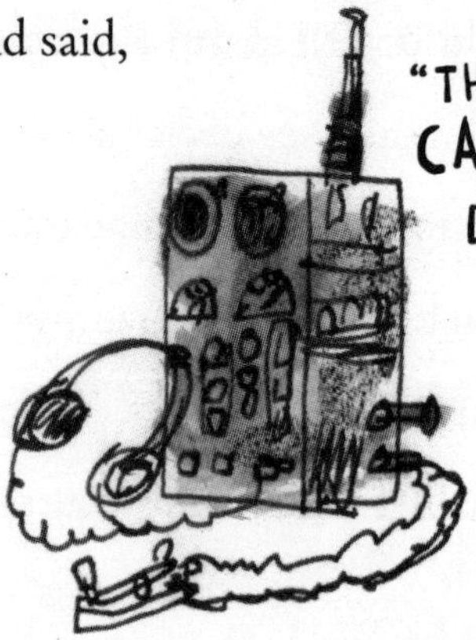

The Queen bowed her head.

Alfred thought he recognised that voice, but he couldn't be sure. A voice from his dim and distant past, perhaps.

"*Regina*. The Latin word for Queen," began the Lord Protector. "Hundreds of coded messages going back and forth over the last few weeks. Here, in the throne room, we intercepted them all. Then tonight, moments after your last message, KABOOM!

Another precious building in flames. Sickening. Absolutely sickening."

Alfred couldn't believe it, didn't want to believe it, but he knew from the look on his mother's face that it was true.

"Mama? How could you? The **revolutionaries** are evil! They want to kill us all!" he exclaimed.

"I can explain," she spluttered, turning to the King. "My darling husband, you've changed. Something has happened to you, something very wrong, and I don't know what. Please, I beg you. Don't do this!"

The Lord Protector turned to the King. "Your Majesty, what would you like me to do with the traitor?"

Alfred was stunned into silence as that dreaded word sank in. TRAITOR.

"Take her to the Tower," ordered the King.

"NO!" screamed the Queen. "Henry, it's me, your wife. The mother of your child. I love you. Why are you doing this to me? Or is this really all the work of the Lord Protector? He has you under some kind of spell!"

On the Lord Protector's nod, the royal guards seized her arms tightly and began dragging her out of the room.

"MAMA!" cried Alfred, and he reached out to grab her hand. But, before he could, a guard shoved him away.

"ARGH!"

The boy fell to the floor.

THUD!

"You are now the kingdom's only hope," said the Queen. "Goodbye, *Lionheart!*"

Alfred watched as the huge metal doors to the throne room slid open…

WHOOSH!

…and closed behind her.

His mother was gone. Perhaps forever.

The Lord Protector paced over to the prince. "There, there," he said, reaching out to comfort him.

"No. I don't want you. I want Mama back. PLEASE! I BEG YOU!"

"Your Royal Highness, I realise this is deeply upsetting news, that your mother, the Queen, is a traitor. But I want you to know that I am always here for you. I am, and will forever be, your loyal servant. If you need to talk about your feelings, you know my door is always open, as it has been for your father."

"Please leave me now," said the King, still staring off into space. "I need to be alone."

"Of course, Your Majesty," replied the Lord Protector. He took the prince tightly by the hand. "This must be a difficult time for you more than any of us."

Still holding the boy

tightly by the hand, he made his way over to the metal door.

"Father?" said Alfred, turning towards the King.

"Please, you heard His Majesty – your father needs to be alone," said the Lord Protector.

"Mama is a good person," said the boy. "The best. If she did this, there must be a reason."

"The reason is that there is evil inside her," interjected the Lord Protector. "The Tower of London is the best place for her. The Executioner should be able to cast the evil out. By hook or by crook."

Alfred gulped. Whatever "by hook or by crook" meant, it sounded deadly.

No one sent to the Tower of London ever came back.

"Now come on, young prince, a sickly child like you shouldn't be out of bed at this late hour. You might catch your death," said the Lord Protector. "You will be King yourself one day. We wouldn't want anything happening to you, now, would we?"

The huge metal door slid open…

WHOOSH!

…and he led the boy out of the throne room.

Alfred allowed himself one last glimpse of his father. He was searching for a flicker of kindness in his eyes. A shadow of the man he used to be.

But there

was

nothing.

CHAPTER 5

Unblinking Stare

As the Lord Protector led him slowly along the corridor, Alfred could sense something hovering behind.

He looked round to see a giant eye staring back at him. It was the All-Seeing Eye, a huge roving robot camera.

It was powered by thousands of tiny jets, which allowed it to move silently in any direction.

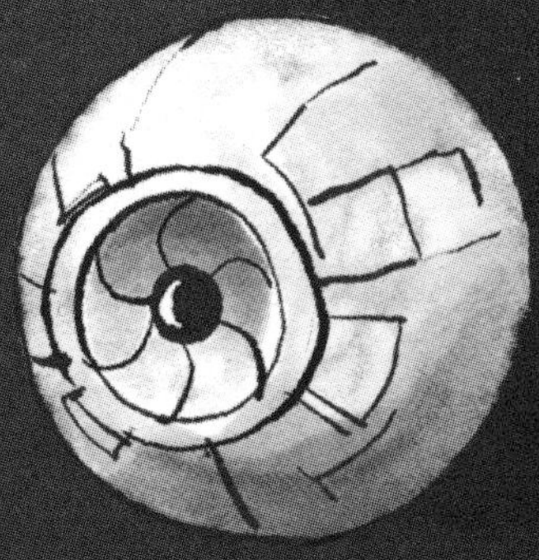

Up.

Down.

Left.

Right.

And everything in between.

The All-Seeing Eye could soar high up into the air above the palace to see for miles around, or glide silently down into the depths of the building.

What it saw through its unblinking eye was beamed right back to that huge television screen in the throne room. There the King, and of course the Lord Protector, could see **EVERYTHING.**

Nothing and nobody could escape its unblinking stare.

Alfred was drained, not just physically but also emotionally. It took all his strength to climb the long, winding staircase back up to his room at the top of the palace.

When he finally reached his bedroom, the Lord Protector said, "Goodnight, Your Royal Highness. I know how much you love a good book. Would you care for a goodnight story?"

"No," came the terse reply. "I am not a baby."

The boy's eyes were still stinging with tears.

"Forgive me, sir, but you do sometimes cry like one."

Alfred wanted to thump him. If only he had the strength.

"Just a little joke, sir. There's no point shedding tears over traitors. After you," purred the Lord Protector, guiding the young prince through the doorway with a little bow.

Then, with the precision and speed of a close-up

magician, he took the key from out of the lock on the inside.

"I think it best I hold on to this, sir, for your own protection, of course," he said.

"But–!"

"I wish you goodnight. Sweet dreams."

The Lord Protector patted him on the head. Alfred couldn't bear the man's long, thin fingers touching him. He shuddered.

With the All-Seeing Eye still hovering behind, the Lord Protector shut the prince's bedroom door and locked it.

CLICK!

Alfred staggered to his bed and lay down, burying his head in the pillow.

He wanted to cry until his body turned inside out. Just like a baby.

But, right now,

tears

solved

nothing.

Alfred had to do something.

He sat up on the bed. From his window he could see that St Paul's Cathedral was still ablaze. By morning this historic monument, an icon of London's skyline, would be little more than charred rubble.

In his heart, the boy knew that his mother couldn't be behind this terrible attack. It went against everything he knew about her, and he knew her better than anybody. She was kind and loving, the best mother he could ever imagine. The Queen was not capable of such unspeakable horror. What's more, why would she ever do such a thing?

The **revolutionaries** were the sworn enemies of the royals. They wanted the royal family dead. **It didn't make sense.**

Alfred was determined to find out what was really going on.

The mysterious chalk markings on the floor.

The strange cuts on his father's hands.

His dearest mama being branded a traitor.

It *couldn't* be true.

Alfred was determined to prove his mother's innocence.

To do that he had to turn detective.

The boy tiptoed back over to his bedroom door. Peeping through the crack under it, he could see a shadow on the floor. The All-Seeing Eye was still hovering outside, keeping watch over him. Even if he could find a way of unlocking the door, royal guards would be here in seconds. His next stop would be the Tower of London.

Instead, Alfred tiptoed over to his window.

As the glory days of Buckingham Palace were long gone, in the prince's bedroom there was an infestation of woodworm – the larvae of beetles that eat through wood. There were tiny holes in his bedframe, his cupboard and, when he rolled back the stained silk rug that lay in the middle of his room, there were holes in the floorboards too.

The window frames were made of wood, and the wood was rotting. Alfred ran his fingers along the hundreds of little holes in the frame. Cold air was whistling through them. That meant that, even though the glass was bulletproof, there might be a way of taking the whole window out.

Alfred crept over to his wardrobe. He pulled a wire coat hanger off the rail.

CLANK!

Next, he untwisted it…

RINK! DINK! KINK!

…then bent it so he was left with a long metal rod. He made sure the end had a little bend in it, then fed it through one of the tiny holes. Next, he grabbed another coat hanger…

CLANK!

…and did the same to a hole below. Then another two on the other side of the window, top and bottom.

Now, already feeling the worse for wear, Alfred gathered up the ends of all four coat hangers in his hand and pulled. At first nothing happened. No wonder. It was a real struggle for the boy to muster any strength in his thin little arms. Alfred took a deep breath and pulled again. Harder this time. Still nothing. Then he closed his eyes, and yanked the ends of the coat hangers as hard as he possibly could.

SUCCESS!

The whole window came loose. Now a huge slab of glass was coming straight towards him!

WHOOSH!

It was so heavy it could flatten him.

Just in time, he caught it in his hands.

CHONK!

"OOF!"

Immediately Alfred realised he wasn't strong enough to keep holding it, and so lowered it to the floor as slowly and silently as he could.

THUNK!

A blast of cold air swept into his bedroom.

WHISH!

Alfred hadn't breathed air from the outside for as long as he could remember.

Next, he peered out. There was a drainpipe on the wall within arm's reach that he might be able to climb down. However, he couldn't just leave the window frame lying there. A missing window on the side of Buckingham Palace would arouse suspicion. So, he righted it, swapped the coat hangers to the other side, and stepped out on to the slippery windowsill.

Suddenly, it dawned on Alfred that it was an awfully long way down from the top of the palace to the bottom. If he lost his grip, he'd be nothing more than human jam.*

---

* Human jam is considered to be the most revolting of all the jams. Other unpopular varieties include:

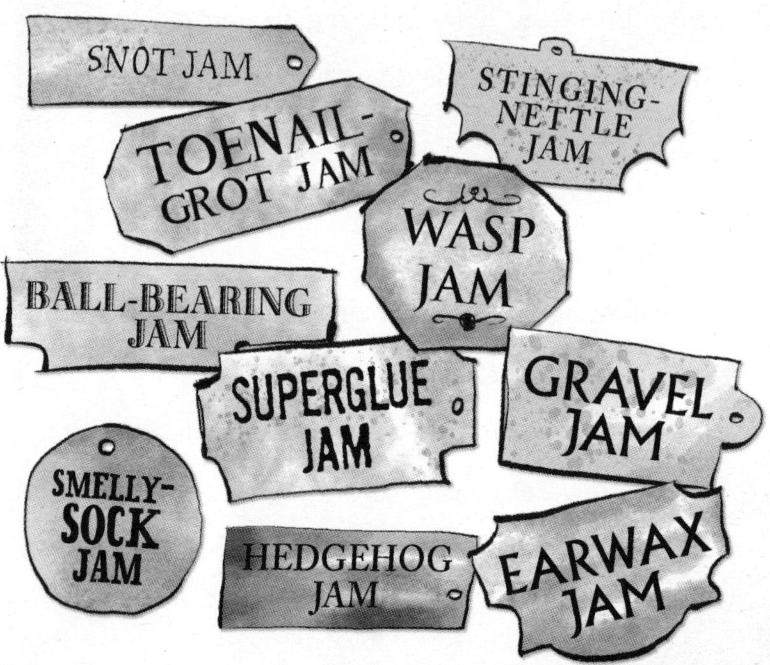

Next, using his weight as a lever, he pulled the window back into place from the outside.

SHTONK!

Then, summoning all his strength, Alfred shimmied over to the drainpipe.

Avoiding the royal guards' searchlights that raked the walls day and night looking for intruders, the boy slid over to the side.

Right next to his room was the King's bedroom. He and the Queen had had separate bedrooms for as long as Alfred could remember.

The room was vast, with a huge four-poster bed, two sofas arranged around a coffee table and a marble

fireplace. From outside the window, Alfred saw his father sitting alone on the end of his bed. The man stared straight ahead. At first Alfred was worried that his father had glimpsed him. But no. The man was staring into space.

The King rubbed the palms of his hands. That is where those strange cuts were.

Just then, the door to the King's bedroom opened.

CLICK!

It was the Lord Protector. Alfred ducked out of view.

Then, after a few moments, the boy lifted his head so he could peer through the window again.

He could see the Lord Protector leading his father off somewhere. **But where?**

As the King's bedroom door closed behind them, Alfred began his

slow

descent

down

the

drainpipe.

The next window was the library. This was one of the largest rooms in the palace, stocked from top to bottom with antique books, all of them extraordinary. Some even unique.

ANCIENT ENGLAND
HERALDRY THROUGH THE AGES
A HISTORY OF ROYAL PALACES
A BOOK OF DRAGONS
THE CROWN JEWELS
THE ENGLISH CIVIL WAR
ROYAL PORTRAITURE
AN ENCYCLOPEDIA OF TRAITORS

NOTABLE BEHEADINGS
Witchcraft of the British Isles
ROYAL TOILETS
SMELLS OF MEDIEVAL BRITAIN: A SCRATCH-&-SNIFF BOOK

Alfred was surprised NOT to see the Lord Protector in the library. He was often to be found there alone, reading late into the night. The library was where the man had begun his career at Buckingham Palace, all those years ago when he was just a humble librarian. This was decades before he became Lord Protector.

There was a narrow gap in the curtains, and Alfred manoeuvred himself closer to the glass, so he could peek through.

The lights were out, and the room was dark.

But the light of a candle flickered in the gloom.

There was a lone figure with their back to the window. Who were they? And what were they doing?

It was hard to make out. Alfred kept very still and watched.

Someone was trying to force open the cabinet that held the most special books. Frantically, though. As if their life depended on it.

Alfred pressed his face right up against the window to get a better look, but as he did so he lost his footing for a moment, and his head hit the glass.

THUNK!

Immediately, the candle was blown out, and the library was plunged into darkness.

Alfred moved out of sight of the window.

Just then a searchlight came towards him.

Were the royal guards going to shoot him from the ground?

Alfred stayed as still as the stone gargoyle right next to him on the wall of the palace as the searchlight passed over him. The prince didn't even dare take a breath.

Then he heard the sound of the window opening.

SHUNT!

Just as he tried to hurry back up the drainpipe, a hand reached out of the window, and yanked him inside.

"ARGH!" he screamed.

CHAPTER 6

Dead of Night

"What are you doing out there in the dead of night?" demanded a voice.

Alfred was lying on the floor of the palace library with a figure looming over him. He knew that voice better than his own.

"Nanny?"

"SHUSH!" she shushed.

"It *is* you."

"Yes, I know it's me. You know it's me. But we don't need the whole wide world knowing about it."

"What are you doing here?" asked the boy, scrambling to his feet.

"I asked first," replied Nanny.

This lady must have had a name, but everyone

called her "Nanny". The plump and cheery old girl was in her eighties. She was so old that she'd been alive when there was still sunlight over Britain. Before the darkness came.

Nanny had looked after two generations of royal children: the prince and his father, the King. As a result, she was one of the most trusted members of the royal household. Needless to say, Nanny was the person you would least expect to see up to no good in the dead of night.

"Well," began Alfred, "I was looking for something."

"What?"

"I don't know."

"How can you look for something when you don't know what you are looking for?"

"That's a good question," he replied. "I think I'll know when I find it. Now, what are you doing here?"

"Just browsing."

"Browsing?"

"I'm looking for a book."

"What book?"

Nanny quickly changed the subject. "Look at you! You'll catch your death. A sickly child like you abseiling down Buckingham Palace dressed only in your pyjamas! You must have gone bananas! Now come here, *my little prince!*"

The lady drew the boy close and gave him a big hug. Instantly, she could feel how cold he was. Alfred looked over her shoulder and saw that ***The Book of Albion*** was not in its usual place in the cabinet. Instead, it was on a pile of books on a small table. He thought that was strange, but said nothing.

"Ooh! You're frozen solid!" continued Nanny. "We'll have to put you straight in a steaming-hot bath. Now come on…"

"No," replied the prince.

"What do you mean, 'no'?"

"I haven't come this far to be put in the bath."

"Shower?"

"No!"

"Sink?"

"No!"

"Bidet?"*

"No!" barked the boy. Why on earth would he need a bidet at this moment in time?

"I'm looking for an answer!" stated Alfred.

"An answer to what?" asked Nanny.

"To why my mother was taken to the Tower."

Nanny shook her head and tutted. "Ooh yes, I heard your poor mother being dragged away. Shouting and screaming, she was. I tried to stop the guards."

"You did?" asked Alfred.

"Oh yes! I gave them a piece of my mind and no mistake! Even jumped on the back of one!"

"What happened?"

The old lady shook her head sorrowfully.

"I was no match for them. Must have been six of them taking her off. They threw me to the floor."

"Oh no, Nanny. Are you all right?"

"Black and blue, I am," she said, rubbing her arms. "But Nanny's a tough old bird. I will survive." She smiled, showing off her false teeth that went

---

* If you don't know what a bidet is, ask someone French, or someone with a really stinky bottom. Or, better still, someone French with a really stinky bottom.

CLICKETY-CLACK whenever she spoke.

"Do you believe Mama could really be a TRAITOR?"

Nanny sighed heavily. "It seems far-fetched, but you never know. Sometimes the enemy is closer than you think."

This sent shivers down the boy's spine.

"What do you mean?" he asked.

"I mean, maybe, just maybe, it's true."

Alfred felt sick at the thought. Mama, a TRAITOR?

"Now come on, *my little prince*. You're not a well boy. You need to get straight to bed. And double helpings of Nanny's special **eggy-wegg** in the morning."

Alfred gulped. He didn't much like Nanny's special **eggy-wegg**. Even though he'd been given them every single day of his life he didn't have the heart to tell her. There were no fresh eggs in the palace, or indeed anywhere any more, so these scrambled **eggy-weggs** were made with powdered egg. They tasted funny. Funny peculiar, not funny ha ha.*

---

* IT WOULD BE WEIRD IF EGGS TASTED HILARIOUS.

"I am not going to bed!" announced the boy, before yawning. The events of the night had left him absolutely shattered, but he was determined to fight on.

"Yes, you are. Straight to bed, young man, and no arguing!"

"BUT—!"

Suddenly Nanny stood very still. A noise had distracted her. She brought her finger up to her lips to silence him. Then, with her eyes, she indicated the door at the far end of the library. Alfred tiptoed over to it, and then bent to peer through the keyhole.

Nanny was right. There was someone or something out there. He put his little eye up to the keyhole and found a giant eye staring back at him.

"Huh!" the boy gasped.

"SHUSH!" shushed Nanny, as quietly as she could shush.

The All-Seeing Eye was hovering outside the door. Alfred felt a wave of fear CRASH over him.

He didn't move and eventually the eye hovered off down the long corridor.

Alfred waited until it was a safe distance away, before tiptoeing past the shelves and shelves of books back to Nanny.

"Who was it?" she whispered.

"It was the Eye," whispered Alfred.

"Oh, I can't bear that great big nosy beachball! I once caught it spying on me when I was on the lavvy! Dirty blighter! Did it see you?"

"I don't know," said the boy with a gulp.

"Well, did it, or didn't it?" she pressed, clearly concerned.

"I don't know. Maybe."

"Maybe!" she fretted. "Then maybe we will both be sent to the Tower! We need to get out of here. And fast!"

"Should I go back the way I came in?"

"THE WINDOW? No, no, no!" snapped Nanny. "You are lucky the guards didn't see you. Someone scaling the wall of the palace at night! You could have been blasted from here to Timbuktu!"

"Then how?"

Just then, they heard the handle on the door to the library turn.

CLICK!

Someone was about to

march in.

CHAPTER 7

The Room With No Door

The old lady grabbed the prince by the hand, so he was standing right next to her at the library fireplace. Before Alfred could ask Nanny what she was doing, she turned the little hand of the gold carriage clock on top of the fireplace anticlockwise.

WHIRR!

As if by magic, the pair were spun into another room.

WHOOSH!

"I never knew this room was here," hissed Alfred.

"SHUSH!" shushed Nanny. "They still might hear us."

They listened out for voices in the library next door, as they stood in a tiny windowless room full of junk.

There was a rusty metal bath, a broken bicycle, a dog-chewed cricket bat, a weather-beaten picnic basket, a mouldy croquet set and a battered old Victorian pram with a wonky wheel. Alfred had been all over the palace, but he had never been in here. Hardly surprising, as the room had no door.

"Is this a secret room?" he whispered.

"SHUSH!" shushed Nanny.

There were a couple of old, chipped cut-glass tumblers on a side table. Nanny picked one up and passed the other to the boy. She then placed the top of the tumbler to the wall, and the bottom to her ear.

Alfred followed suit. Next door they could hear someone pacing around the library. Who was it? What were they looking for? Whoever it was, and whatever they were looking for, at last it sounded as if they'd found it. After a short while, the pair heard the library door close. They were safe. For now.

"In answer to your question, *my little prince*," began Nanny, "legend has it that there are many secret rooms and passages all over Buckingham Palace. I know of just a few."

"They must have been built here during World War Two!"

"Yes! For the royal family back then, in case that stinker Hitler invaded."

"King George the Sixth!"

"Oh, *my little prince*, you've been reading all those books piled up in your bedroom."

"History books are my favourite."

"I know!"

"George the Sixth had a wife and two daughters," continued the boy. "The elder one became Elizabeth the Second."

"Full marks, clever clogs! Elizabeth the Second. What a ruler she was. We'll never see her like again."

Prince Alfred, who was next in line to the throne,

nodded his head sorrowfully. He knew more than anyone of his failings. If only he could be more like the great kings and queens of the past. But nature had played him a cruel trick. He was a sickly child.

All of a sudden, Alfred thought he saw something **move** under an old dustsheet.

With his eyes, he indicated the pile.

Nanny mimed, "What?"

Whatever it was **moved** again.

Nanny nodded and began tiptoeing over to the sheet. The boy stayed close behind, holding on to her cardigan for dear life.

The sheet rose into the air. It looked like a ghost. Alfred wanted to scream, but didn't dare make a sound.

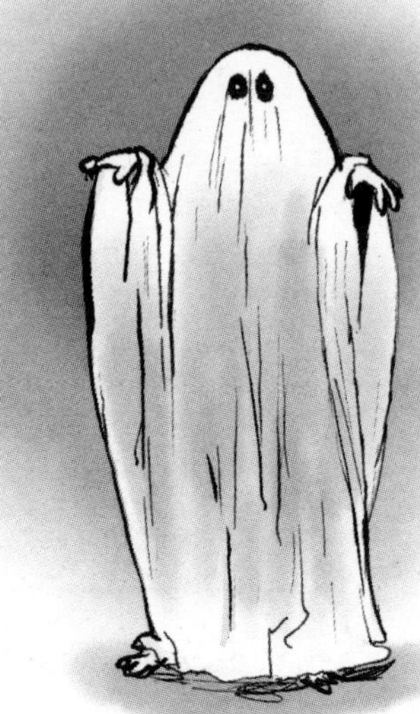

The thing stretched out its arms.

Nanny reached out her hand and closed her eyes. She couldn't bear it either. With one hand, she

whipped off

the sheet to reveal…

CHAPTER 8

Prince of Nothing

A little girl.

Dressed in rags. Her face, hands and feet blackened with dirt. She was a pathetic sight.

"All right?" chirped the girl.

"Who are *you*?" demanded Alfred.

"Who are *you*?" she asked back.

"I asked first."

"What do you think you're doing sneaking in here from the outside?" demanded Nanny. "Well?"

Alfred noticed that the girl was pongy. Pongy was putting it politely. Pongy is low on the **STINKY** SCALE.

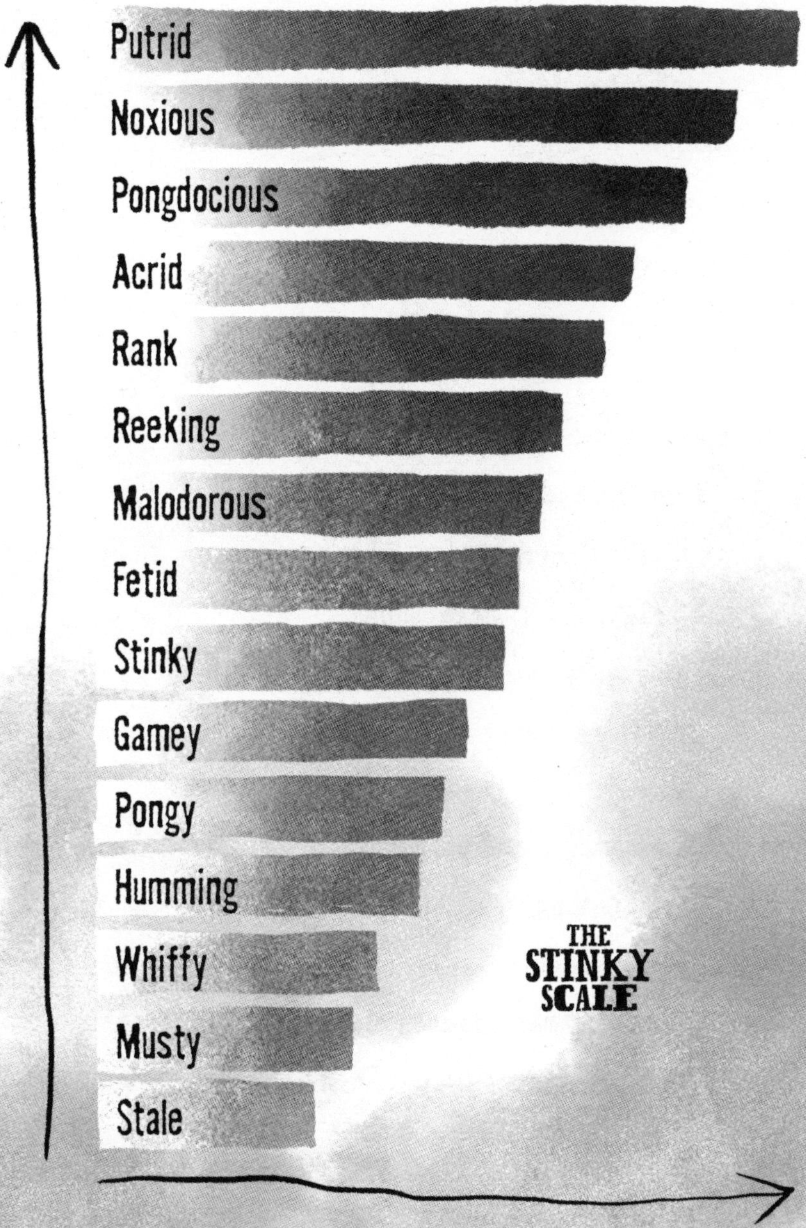

THE STINKY SCALE

Putrid

Noxious

Pongdocious

Acrid

Rank

Reeking

Malodorous

Fetid

Stinky

Gamey

Pongy

Humming

Whiffy

Musty

Stale

However, being well brought up, Alfred was far too polite to mention that the little girl **smelled** something rotten.

Nanny snatched a broken candelabra and brandished it like a weapon.

"Don't beat me!" pleaded the girl.

"How do we know you're not one of the **revolutionaries?"** demanded Nanny.

"I am not. I swear."

Alfred noticed the girl was dripping wet.

"You're soaked!" he exclaimed.

"How did you get into Buckingham Palace?" said Nanny. "This place is a fortress. Come on! Out with it!"

"I swam."

"Nonsense!" scoffed Nanny.

"No, it ain't," snapped the girl. "Years ago, there was all these trains that ran under the city."

"THE LONDON UNDERGROUND?" replied Alfred. "I have a book on it upstairs in my room. It hasn't run for fifty years."

"Yeah. Most of the tunnels collapsed ages ago, but

there is one that is all flooded."

"Flooded?" asked the boy.

"Yeah. This tunnel is underwater. Leads all the way from the Thames to right under the palace."

"Well, in all my years of working here I never knew that," remarked the old lady.

"It's a secret," hissed the girl. "Nobody knows."

"Well, I know now," replied Nanny.

"Me too!" added Alfred.

"Silly girl," said Nanny.

But the girl was not going to be mocked like this. "You don't know exactly where it is, though, do ya?" she retorted, before a smug grin settled on her face.

Alfred smirked. This little one had spirit!

"What's your name?" he asked.

"Mite."

"Might what?"

"No, just Mite."

"Might as in M I G H T or as in M I T E?"

"I dunno spelling. They call me 'Mite' cos I'm a little mite."

"That's M I T E," he said.

The girl just shrugged her shoulders, as if to say, "I don't care."

"You still haven't told us why you've broken into Buckingham Palace!" snapped Nanny.

Mite gulped. "I was starvin'. My belly hurts something horrible with the hunger. I was looking for the kitchen to rob some food, then I heard footsteps and hid in here."

"Did you not have your dinner?" asked Alfred.

"Dinner?" she exclaimed. "What planet are you on? A nibble of a mouldy old biscuit is all I've had all day!"

"Really?" The prince was flabbergasted.

"You have absolutely no idea about life outside this place, do ya?"

"Well, I er…"

"In here, you've got everything. Outside we've got nothing. The story is there's mountains and mountains of food in this palace, but the King just won't share it," continued Mite. "Stuff I've only ever dreamed of. Cakes and sweets and chocolate!" she said, her eyes gleefully lighting up at the thought.

"Don't have the **eggy-wegg**," offered Alfred.

Nanny gave the boy a filthy look.

"Well, I'm sure we can give you some food," he added.

"We will do no such thing!" huffed Nanny. "We don't want to encourage her. First it's her, then we will be swamped by the great unwashed! No! She is very lucky not to have been shot on sight by the guards."

"Shot or starved to death," mused Mite. "I was willing to take me chances. You don't know what it's like out there. That's why one day there is going to be a revolution!"

"I have heard quite enough of this!" snapped Nanny.

"I'm sure there is something we can do to help all those on the outside," said Alfred.

"Oh yeah? What are you going to do, then, posh boy?"

Alfred stammered. "Well, I, er…"

The truth was, he didn't have the faintest idea.

"Who are ya anyway?" she asked.

"You don't know?" spluttered the prince.

"Should I?"

"I am the prince!" he announced grandly. As if there were no other way to announce you were royalty.

"Prince of what?" asked the girl.

"Prince of..." For once the prince was lost for words.

"Prince of Nothing!" she announced.

Judging by the look on Nanny's face, she had heard quite enough.

"How dare you be so rude!" snapped Nanny.

"It's true! No one out there has seen you royals for years. All we see is the face of this Lord Protector. Goodness knows what he's up to!"

"I don't want to hear another word out of you!" chided Nanny. "You show me where this underground river thingy is, and I'll let you go."

The girl thought for a moment. "I'll show you where it is if you give me some chocolate!"

"The cheek of it!" exclaimed Nanny.

"Please, Nanny," implored Alfred. "Let's give Mite some chocolate. And some for her family."

"I don't have any family. Me mum and dad were shot by the royal guards when I was only three."

"Oh no," whispered Alfred. "I am so sorry."

"I am sorry too."

"There must have been a reason," said Nanny. "Perhaps they were **revolutionaries?**"

"They were shot for stealing a loaf of bread."

Alfred was shocked to his core. So this was what his country had become!

"That's evil!" he said.

"Show me how you got into the palace," said Nanny, changing the subject, "and I will bring you the biggest bar of chocolate you could ever imagine."

"I can imagine a really big bar! Like ginormous!"

"Then show me where you broke into the palace. RIGHT. NOW."

The little girl looked at her with suspicion in her eyes. "I don't trust you, old lady. I don't trust you one bit."

"Nanny has looked after me my whole life!" announced Alfred, jumping to her defence. "I couldn't **trust** her more!"

Mite looked the boy up and down. "And I don't trust you either, Prince of Nothing! I'll find me own chocolate!"

With that, she threw the dustsheet over their heads.

Alfred and Nanny coughed and spluttered in all the dust. When they'd pulled the sheet off, the girl was gone.

"Mite?" called out Alfred. "Mite?"

They paced around the junk room, but there was no sign of the little girl anywhere. She had simply disappeared. Perhaps

she

was

a ghost,

after

all...

CHAPTER 9

Festering

"What a nasty little wretch!" was Nanny's verdict.

"She was just hungry," reasoned Alfred.

"She's a thief, young man. And thieves like her belong in the Tower."

The prince wasn't so sure. She was only a child like him. And she was hungry. It wasn't right that the people of Britain lived like that.

"Now, *my little prince*, we need to get you back to your bedroom."

Alfred didn't want to go back. Being in his bedroom was boring, and he had detective work to do.

"Not now, Nanny!"

"Yes now! The question is, how?"

Alfred peered around the room of junk, and spotted a bicycle. "Could I cycle back?"

Nanny did not look convinced. "Do you know how to ride a bike?"

"No."

"Well, I would say no, then. Not really time for lessons right now."

"No."

The pair fell silent for a moment, before the old lady exclaimed, "Oh! Nanny has an idea! And it's a goody!"

"What?"

"Hide in that old pram."

"The *pram*?" Now it was Alfred's turn to look unconvinced.

"YES!"

"I am *not* getting into a pram."

"You never used to complain!"

"That was when I was a baby! What use is the pram anyway?"

"I can pretend I am using it to wheel some clean

blankets up to your bedroom."

"At this late hour?"

"I'll say you've wet the bed."

Alfred was not impressed. He hadn't wet the bed for… well, a long, long time.

He peered into the pram. It was full of festering old blankets that must have been damp for decades. Now they had things growing on them. And the things growing on *them* had things growing on *them*! And the things growing on *them* had things growing on *them* too!

"In there?" he asked, incredulous.

"Yes. In there."

"You mean actually inside the pram?"

"Yes, of course inside, you great nit!"

"But it STINKS!"

"Stinky is better than dead! Now come on, climb in!"

In truth, the smell was RANK, which is higher up the **STINKY** SCALE than **STINKY**.

The old lady smiled an expectant smile. Alfred sighed and with real difficulty clambered into

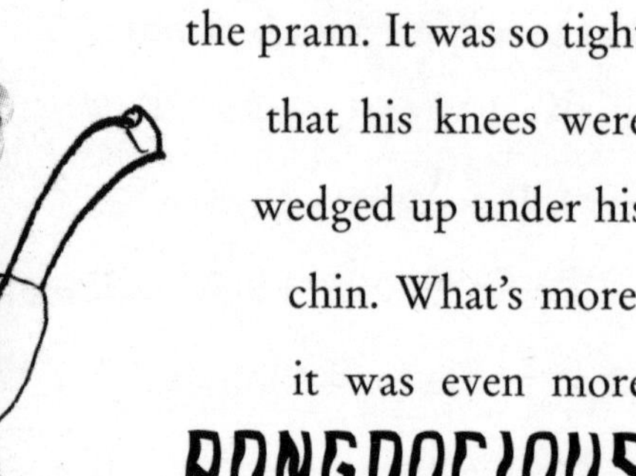

the pram. It was so tight that his knees were wedged up under his chin. What's more, it was even more **PONGDOCIOUS** than he had first thought. The smell was positively medieval, which may have been the era when those blankets had last been washed.

"I'm in!" said Alfred, covering his mouth for fear he might barf.

"I'd better cover you up!" said Nanny, pulling a musty old blanket over his head.

Now he really felt he might barf.

"So, Alfred, remember not to sneeze, cough or you know what," ordered Nanny.

"No, I don't know what."

"Bottom burp."

"Oh yes."

"Or you'll give the game away. Ready, *my little prince?*"

"No!" he replied, pulling the cover back.

"Ah!" cooed Nanny. "You look like you did when you were a baby!"

Alfred didn't find that the least bit amusing.

"The Lord Protector!" he remembered. "He locked my bedroom door from the outside. We won't be able to get in!"

"Don't you worry. Nanny always carries a spare key!" she said, fishing it out of her cardigan pocket.

"Clever Nanny!"

"Now, come on, little baby, back to sleep!" She snorted to herself, her teeth going CLICKETY-CLACK in her mouth.

In a grump now, Alfred pulled the revolting blanket back over his head.

As soon as he had, the old lady wheeled the pram to the correct spot on the floor of the junk room. She turned the hand on the carriage clock anticlockwise, and the pair spun round into the library.

CHAPTER 10

Metal Menace

Looking up from the pram, Alfred asked, "What book was that person looking for at this late hour?"

"I don't have a clue!" replied Nanny.

"You were looking for a book here in the library too, Nanny."

"Was I?"

"Yes! What was the name of it?"

"SHUSH!" shushed Nanny. "Or someone will hear us!"

With that she wheeled the pram out of the library and down one of the palace's long sweeping corridors. The wonky wheel made it difficult to steer...

SQUEAK! SQUEAK! SQUEAK!

...and Nanny kept on bashing the pram into the wall.

BONK!

"OW!" complained the boy.

"SHUSH!" shushed Nanny again. Louder this time. The SHUSH was so loud it was hardly a shush at all.

SQUEAK! SQUEAK! SQUEAK!

Then she bashed the pram into the wall again.

BONK!

SQUEAK! SQUEAK! SQUEAK!

And again.

BONK!

Alfred grimaced. At this rate, he'd be lucky to get back to his bedroom alive.

Next, he heard the sound of something trundling.

Oh no, he thought. *Not the* OCTOBUT*!* That's the last thing they needed right now.

"Good morning, Archbishop!" the robot announced.

"Will you be quiet, you blasted thing!" hissed Nanny.

"I have warmed your socks, so they're nice and toasty!"

The boy thought he could smell burning.

"Out of my way, you metal menace!" said the old lady.

CRASH!

Next, Alfred could feel the wheels of the pram BUMP over something.

CLANK!

Something metal.

He looked past Nanny and saw that the accident-prone robot had lost yet another one of its arms. The one with the little spoon attached for stirring tea was now lying twitching on the floor.

TWITCH!
TWITCH!
TWITCH!

Down to five arms, the OCTOBUT could now be called a Quinquebut, but that just sounds silly.

"I will post your boiled egg on to you!" it called out after them.

"Shush!" shushed Nanny before pushing the prince's head back into the pram. "Get down!"

As he was wheeled around the palace, Alfred listened intently. He was trying to work out from sounds around him where exactly he was. All of a sudden, he could feel the pram being heaved up the sweeping staircase that led all the way from the bottom of the palace to the top.

SHUNT!

SHUNT!

SHUNT!

SHUNT!

"Nanny! There must be hundreds of stairs!" he protested.

"Shush!" she shushed. "Someone might hear you!"

SHUNT!

SHUNT!

SHUNT!

SHUNT!

"We are never going to make it!"

"I said shush!"

SHUNT!

SHUNT!

SHUNT!

"Nanny, I'm scared you're going to let go!"

"I will if you don't shut up!"

SHUNT!

SHUNT!

SHUNT!

SHUNT!

Now they were halfway up the staircase.

All of a sudden, Alfred heard a voice.

"Nanny?" said the voice.

Not just any voice.

It was the Lord Protector's voice.

CHAPTER 11

An Ungodly Hour

"Nanny, whatever are you doing out of your room at such an ungodly hour?" purred the Lord Protector.

"Just bringing up some clean blankets, sir," the old lady replied.

Inside the pram, Alfred kept dead still. He could hear in her voice that Nanny was nervous. Her false teeth were CLICKETY-CLACKING in her mouth even more than normal.

"Who were you talking to?" demanded the Lord Protector.

"Myself!" she chirped. "I am a bit barmy like that. Now I must be going..."

SHUNT!

SHUNT!
SHUNT!

"WAIT!" called out the man. "Whatever have you got in that pram?"

Alfred didn't dare breathe.

"Fresh blankets," she replied.

The Lord Protector caught up with her, then leaned down and sniffed.

SNIFF! SNIFF!

"They don't smell fresh," was his verdict.

"Well," Nanny hesitated for a moment, buying herself some time, "they're fresher than the ones I'm changing them for."

"I find that rather difficult to believe."

"Oh, yes, yes, yes, Lord Protector, sir. It's the prince."

"What's the prince?"

"He… erm, how can I put this nicely? He wet the bed."

Inside the pram the prince was *seething*.

"At his age?" asked the Lord Protector.

"Well, it has been a very difficult night for him. What with that terrible business with the Queen."

"Yes, yes," mused the Lord Protector. "What rotten luck having a traitor for a mother."

Alfred wanted to leap up out of the pram and biff the man on the nose. But he stayed put. The truth was he was stuck.

"I've taken the precaution of putting the palace on total lockdown tonight," continued the Lord Protector. "No one, but no one, is allowed out of bed. Not even the King himself. So, as soon as you have changed those blankets, I want you to go straight back to your quarters. Do you understand me?"

"Yes, sir."

"Good. For his own safety, I locked the boy's bedroom door. Here is the key. When you have locked him back in for the night, bring it straight to me."

"Yes, sir."

"Now run along, woman," he ordered.

"Very good, sir."

Alfred listened as the Lord Protector's footsteps echoed down the stairs.

"That was close," hissed the boy from inside the pram.

"I know!" whispered Nanny. "Never mind about you doing a bottom burp, I was so nervous I thought I was going to let one rip that sounded like thunder!"

"Too much information, Nanny."

"A HONKING HURRICANE!"

"Again, Nanny, too much!"

"A TRUMP TORNADO!"

"I got it, Nanny!"

"A BOTTOM BLIZZARD!"

"GOT IT! Now let's get going!"

"Oh yes!"

With that, Nanny continued heaving the pram up the staircase.

SHUNT!

SHUNT!

SHUNT!

SHUNT!

SHUNT!

SHUNT!

He could hear the old lady breathing heavily.

"Are you all right, Nanny?" asked Alfred, poking his head out from under the blankets.

"Yes. Just need to take a rest."

The boy watched as her nose began to wrinkle.

"Are you OK?"

"It's these rotten blankets. I think I am going to… ATISHOO!… sneeze!"

She lifted her hands up to her face and let go of the pram…!

"NANNY!" cried the boy as the pram began bouncing down the staircase.

DONK! DONK!

DONK! DONK!

DONK! DONK!

DONK! DONK!

DONK! DONK!

CHAPTER 12

Runaway Pram

DONK!
DONK!
DONK!
DONK!
DONK!
DONK!
DONK!
DONK!
DONK!
DONK!

The runaway pram was gathering speed

DONK! DONK!
DONK! DONK!
DONK! DONK!
DONK! DONK!
DONK! DONK!

"NOOOOOO!"

cried Nanny from way up the staircase.

"YYYEEESSS!"

cried Alfred from inside the pram, not sure what else to say.

Nanny began running down the staircase after him, but the pram was going so much faster.

DONK! DONK!
DONK! DONK!
DONK! DONK!
DONK! DONK!
DONK! DONK!

Alfred looked up from under the blanket.

Two royal guards on patrol were at the bottom of the stairs. If he didn't die in a pram crash, they were sure to blast him to pieces with their laser guns.

"HELP!" shouted Nanny.

DONK! DONK!
DONK! DONK!
DONK! DONK!
DONK! DONK!
DONK! DONK

The pram was heading straight for the guards.

NOOOOOO! thought Alfred. He closed his eyes, ready for the worst.

DONK! DONK!
DONK! DONK!
DONK! DONK!
DONK! DONK!
DONK! DONK!

Then, STOP! The pram came to a halt. The guards had caught it.

"Ooh, thank you!" cooed Nanny. "Thank you so, so much!"

Alfred opened his eyes. He was alive.

"Now, if you could just carry it back up the stairs for me?"

The prince thought the old lady might be pushing her luck, but to his surprise he felt the pram being lifted and carried up the stairs.

"Ooh, you are strong!" said Nanny admiringly.

Finally, they reached the top of the staircase.

"Thank you kindly!"

said Nanny, and the two royal guards made their way back down the stairs.

"You nearly killed me!" hissed Alfred.

"SHUSH!"

Nanny pushed the pram along the corridor towards the prince's bedroom. With the key the Lord Protector had given her, she unlocked the door, and wheeled the pram inside. As soon as Alfred heard the door shut behind him, he pulled back the rancid blanket, and clambered out of the pram.

"Right, young man! Any time now!" said Nanny. "Oh, you're out already! That was naughty! Now straight to bed!"

"I'm lucky to be alive!"

"Yes! I'm sorry about that. Just had an attack of the... ATISHOO!... sneezes!"

The prince wiped a globule of Nanny's cold, wet snot from his face.

"But thank you for covering for me with the Lord Protector. I know you could get into a lot of trouble."

"Anything for *my little prince*," she said, wobbling his cheek with her hand.

WIBBLE! WOBBLE! WABBLE!

"Now please give me the key," demanded the boy.

"I beg your pardon?" spluttered Nanny.

"The key the Lord Protector gave you. Then I can get out of my room later tonight, to do some more detective work."

"You will do no such thing, Your Royal Highness!"

"I command you to give it to me!"

Nanny was having none of it. "And I command you to go to bed! Right now!"

Reluctantly, Alfred got into his four-poster bed. He sniffed himself.

SNIFF! SNIFF!

"PHEW!" he exclaimed. After hiding under those filthy old blankets, he did not smell good. "I'm very whiffy!"

"Then stop sniffing yourself!" ordered Nanny. "And go to sleep!"

With her fingertips she tenderly stroked his hair.

"Goodnight, little one. I love you!"

"I love you too, Nanny."

"Sleep tight!"

Alfred closed his eyes and listened as she tiptoed out of the room and locked the door behind her.

CLICK!

Sleep? The last thing Alfred wanted to do right now was sleep. His brain was bubbling with a billion thoughts. But he was exhausted. This sickly child had never been out of his bed for this long, and the events of the last few hours had left him feeling spent.

Soon Alfred fell fast asleep,

slipping from one world

of nightmares to another.

CHAPTER 13

Talking Toilet

KNOCK! KNOCK! KNOCK!

It was morning, and Alfred was awoken sharply by a knocking on his bedroom door. But it wasn't someone knocking on the door – it was someone knocking *into* the door.

Or, rather, not some*one* but some*thing*.

Oh no! The OCTOBUT*!* The robot butler was charged with waking the prince up every morning. But all it was doing right now was crashing repeatedly into the door.

KNOCK! KNOCK! KNOCK!

"WAIT, OCTOBUT, WAIT!" It was Nanny's voice. "WAIT! I haven't unlocked the door yet! NAUGHTY OCTOBUT!"

KNOCK! KNOCK! KNOCK!

CLICK!

The old lady opened the bedroom door, precariously balancing the breakfast tray she was carrying in one hand. As soon as the door was fully open, the OCTOBUT trundled SLAP BANG into the doorframe.

DOINK!

Next, it darted into the bookshelf.

SMASH!

The books tumbled to the floor.

THUNK! THUNK! THUNK!

Finally, the OCTOBUT trundled over to the four-poster bed, bumping into a post so hard…

CRUNCH!

...it very nearly made it into a three-poster bed. In doing so, another one of the robot's arms, the one with the duster attached, broke clean off.

SNAP!

The OCTOBUT now only had four of its eight arms left. A Quadributt.

"Good evening, Empress," it announced in its posh robotic voice.

Alfred rolled his eyes. Not again!

"It is time to troop the colour... **MALFUNCTION!** Address the nation... **MALFUNCTION!** Open a library... **MALFUNCTION!"**

"I CAN'T CONTROL IT, SIR!" shouted Nanny over the noise. The old lady was so animated her false teeth were CLICKETY-CLACKING like crazy.

"All right, all right, OCTOBUT!" shouted Alfred. "It is all good, thank you! I am awake!"

"Wake up!" said the robot as the fly swatter on the end of one of its arms whacked the boy repeatedly on the forehead.

THWACK!

"Ouch!"

"MALFUNCTION!"

THWOCK!

"Ouuuch!"

"MALFUNCTION!"

THWUCK!

"Ouuuch!"

"MALFUNCTION!"

"That hurts, you mechanical dustbin!" shouted Alfred.

The next whack hit the boy so hard…

THWAAACK!

…that the fly-swatter arm came clean off.

It fell to the floor with a CLANK!

Three arms left. The OCTOBUT, or rather Tribut, was oblivious.

"If that will be all, I must go and water the curtains... **MALFUNCTION!**... iron the roses... **MALFUNCTION!**... stir the toilet... **MALFUNCTION! MALFUNCTION! MALFUNCTION!**"

With that, the OCTOBUT spun around the prince's bedroom, its remaining arms knocking a table over...

BONK!

...smashing an antique vase to pieces...

CRASH!

...and hurling a statue to the floor...

WALLOP!

"Make it stop!" shouted Alfred.

The no-nonsense nanny threw the plate of food she was still carrying down on the bed, then bashed the robot butler with her antique silver tray.

CLUNK! CLUNK!

CLUNK!

Then she bashed it some more.

CLUNK! CLUNK!

CLUNK!

And some more.

CLUNK! CLUNK!

CLUNK!

"Shoo, you talking toilet!" she shouted.

"Congratulations on your coronation!" were its last words as the old girl shoved the robot out of the bedroom, and slammed the door shut.

THUD!

"Thank goodness for that!" said Alfred.

"I wish that thing had an off button!"

"Any news of my mother?" he asked eagerly.

"None," said Nanny, bowing her head. "I am sorry, *my little prince*. None at all. All I know is that the Queen is being kept prisoner in the Tower of London."

Alfred sat up in bed sharply. ***"Then I need to rescue her."***

CHAPTER 14

Eggy-wegg

Nanny scoffed at the boy's suggestion. "I am afraid that's impossible!"

"Why? Nothing is impossible."

"This is. Outside of Buckingham Palace, the Tower of London is the most heavily guarded building in Britain. It needs to be. It is home to this country's **very worst criminals. Revolutionaries. The worst of the worst.** The most **dangerous** folk. Folk who **want to see you dead."**

A look of panic flashed across the prince's face.

"I pray they don't hurt Mama!" He held on to the old lady's arm. "Oh, Nanny. You must help me. Please! I beg you. Mother is going to come to a grisly end in the Tower unless we do something. And fast."

"There, there!" said Nanny, pulling the young prince to her chest. "Your mother would hate to see you like this, wouldn't she?"

Alfred nodded.

"She wouldn't want you to be sad, now, would she?"

The boy shook his head.

"So come on, eat your breakfast."

Without saying a word, the prince inspected the yellow and orange lump on the chipped china plate. It was, of course...

"**Eggy-wegg!**" exclaimed Nanny.

"Yes. I can see," replied Alfred, trying not to sound too disappointed.

"My special recipe!" boasted the old lady. "Eat up!"

Alfred couldn't face Nanny's **eggy-wegg**. Not this morning.

"I'll have it in a moment, thank you!"

"No, no," she implored. "Eat it all up now. Every last bit. You are not well, *my little prince*. You need to get your strength up."

Nanny settled in on the end of his bed. She smiled at him, and nodded as if to say, *Go on*.

Alfred stared at the scrambled **eggy-wegg**. It looked as if it were plastic and, from experience, it was going to taste like it too. He took a mouthful.

STING!

There was that familiar bitter aftertaste again. Alfred winced. Without swallowing it, he lied, "Delicious! Thank you, Nanny."

"Good boy! Now eat it up while I tidy this room of yours!"

The old lady hopped off the bed and made her way to the window. As she ran her hands over the woodworm holes in the frame, Alfred seized his chance. He spat the mouthful of **eggy-wegg** back on to his plate.

SPLAT!

Then he scooped up the lot and hid it in the drawer of his bedside cabinet.

SHUNT!

"We must get these holes repaired," said Nanny.

"You will catch your death of cold with all this freezing air coming through."

"No, no, Nanny. Please don't," replied Alfred. Without a key, this was his only way out of his bedroom.

"No. No. It has to be done," she said, turning round. At once, she noticed that the boy's plate was empty. "You've finished your **eggy-wegg**!"

"Yes, thank you so much. It was *yummy*."

Immediately, she was suspicious. "That was very quick."

"I was starving."

"Would you like some more **eggy-wegg**?"

"No, no," replied the boy. "I've had exactly the right amount of **eggy-wegg**."

"Good, good," said Nanny. "Now I want you to rest up in bed all day today."

"But what about the Queen?

Oh, Nanny, please! We have to do something!"

"I'll keep my ear to the ground and bring you any news as soon as I have it," she said, sitting next to him on the bed, stroking his head. "I promise. Now back to sleep."

With that, she left the prince's bedroom and locked the door behind her.

CLICK!

Alfred felt as if he were being held prisoner. ***Just like his mother.***

CHAPTER 15

Ruins

Despite not having eaten any of his **eggy-wegg**, Alfred felt more full of life than ever. As soon as Nanny had locked his door, he leaped out of bed. Instantly he began his detective work. He made a big pile on the floor of all his ancient history books. The prince was looking for clues about the markings that had been chalked on the floor of the ballroom.

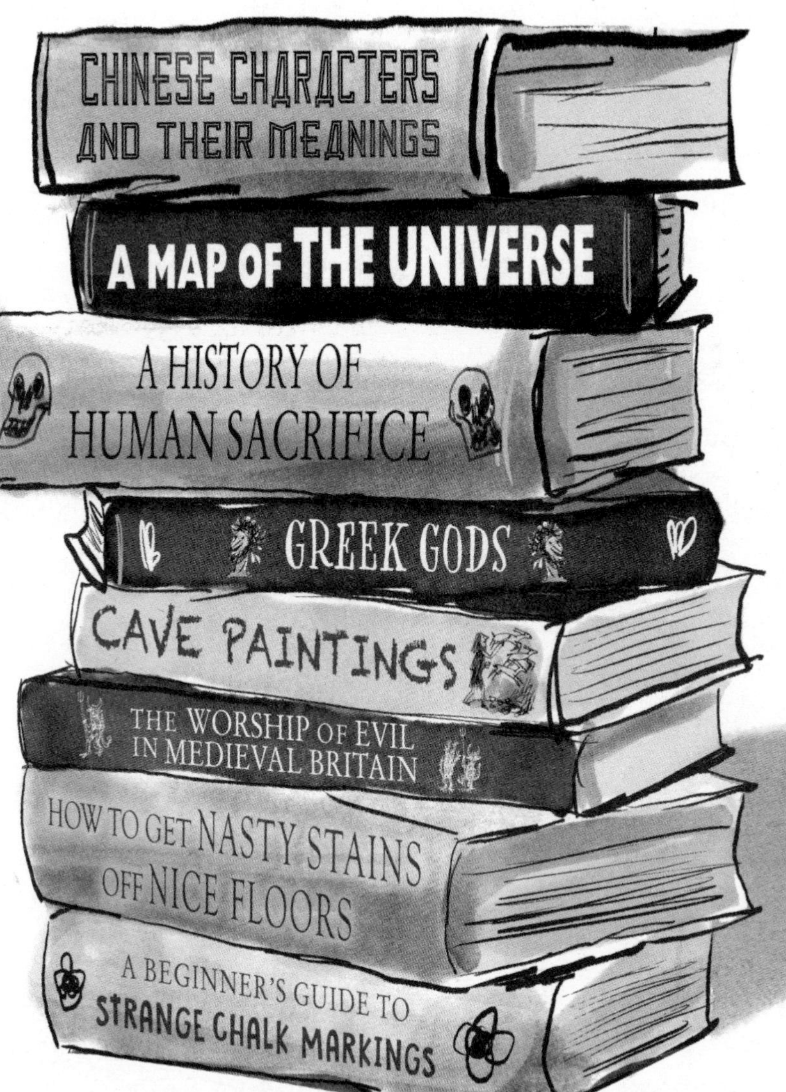

CHINESE CHARACTERS AND THEIR MEANINGS
A MAP OF THE UNIVERSE
A HISTORY OF HUMAN SACRIFICE
GREEK GODS
CAVE PAINTINGS
THE WORSHIP OF EVIL IN MEDIEVAL BRITAIN
HOW TO GET NASTY STAINS OFF NICE FLOORS
A BEGINNER'S GUIDE TO STRANGE CHALK MARKINGS

However much he searched and searched these books, and many others, he couldn't crack the code of what he'd seen on the ballroom floor. The boy needed to take another look, and this time copy down what he saw for reference. Alfred opened the stationery drawer of his antique desk and grabbed a little notepad and a pencil. He stuffed them into his pyjama pocket for safekeeping.

The sound of the siren that rang throughout Buckingham Palace for the beginning of that night's curfew couldn't come soon enough.

WEEOOOOEEE!

This was the time when all those inside the palace had to be safely in their rooms in case of an attack from outside.

Alfred blew out his candle and shuffled over to the window on his knees. The searchlights that scoured the walls of the palace, looking for intruders, passed by his window much more regularly than normal. It was almost as if the royal guards were waiting for him. Alfred didn't dare risk it. The problem was that the only other way out was the door, but that was locked from the outside.

If he were going to carry on his detective work, he'd have to think fast.

Hearing the wind whistle through the fireplace…

WHOOSH!

…Alfred realised this might be the only way out of his bedroom.

So he pulled the grate aside and squeezed his skinny little body up into the flue. It was dark and sooty in there, but because the flue had been made of bricks he could use them to climb up like the rungs of a ladder. As his bedroom was on the top floor, it was only a short climb to the roof of Buckingham

Palace. When he reached the top, he disturbed some pigeons that were nesting there.

SQUAWK! SQUAWK! SQUAWK!

This alerted the royal guards who were keeping watch over London from the roof.

Alfred kept himself hidden inside the chimney as one of the fearsome royal guards left his station to take a closer look. When the last pigeon flew out of the chimney top...

SQUAWK! SQUAWK! SQUAWK!

...the guard returned to his post.

Slowly and silently, the boy climbed out of the top of the chimney. For the first time in his life, he was standing on the roof of Buckingham Palace. As dark clouds swirled above him, he looked out across London. Now he had a 360-degree view of the city. A city that he'd studied in books, one that had the most

Now it was all in ruins.

Alfred thought of what Mite had told him, of the poor people down there, scurrying around in the dark, with little food, and no clean water, surviving from day to day. They were people too, but they had been reduced to living like animals. Only because he'd been born a prince was he here in the palace, and they were down there. No wonder there was talk of revolution. Alfred was beginning to think that maybe the **revolutionaries** weren't the baddies after all. He was determined to do something to help the people of Britain. This was not how the country should be.

Then Alfred heard the sound of something flapping in the wind.

FLIP!

FLAP!

FLUP!

Looking up, he saw the flag of the griffin on top of the flagpole. How he wanted

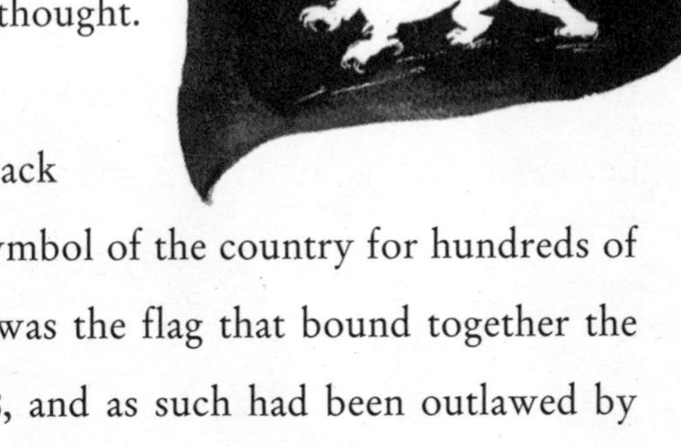

to tear that flag down, and hoist up the Union Jack!

One day, he thought. *One day.*

The Union Jack had been the symbol of the country for hundreds of years. Now it was the flag that bound together the **revolutionaries**, and as such had been outlawed by the Lord Protector.

The black clouds in the sky above Buckingham Palace parted, and a huge airship sailed into view. On its side was the same image of the griffin. This airship was used by the Lord Protector to control the people outside the palace. Right on cue, the projector on the roof of the palace flickered into life. It beamed a shaft of light on to the envelope at the top of the airship, the part that contained all the gas. The envelope was like a cinema screen. An image of a golden griffin appeared, then it faded and was replaced by the face of the Lord Protector.

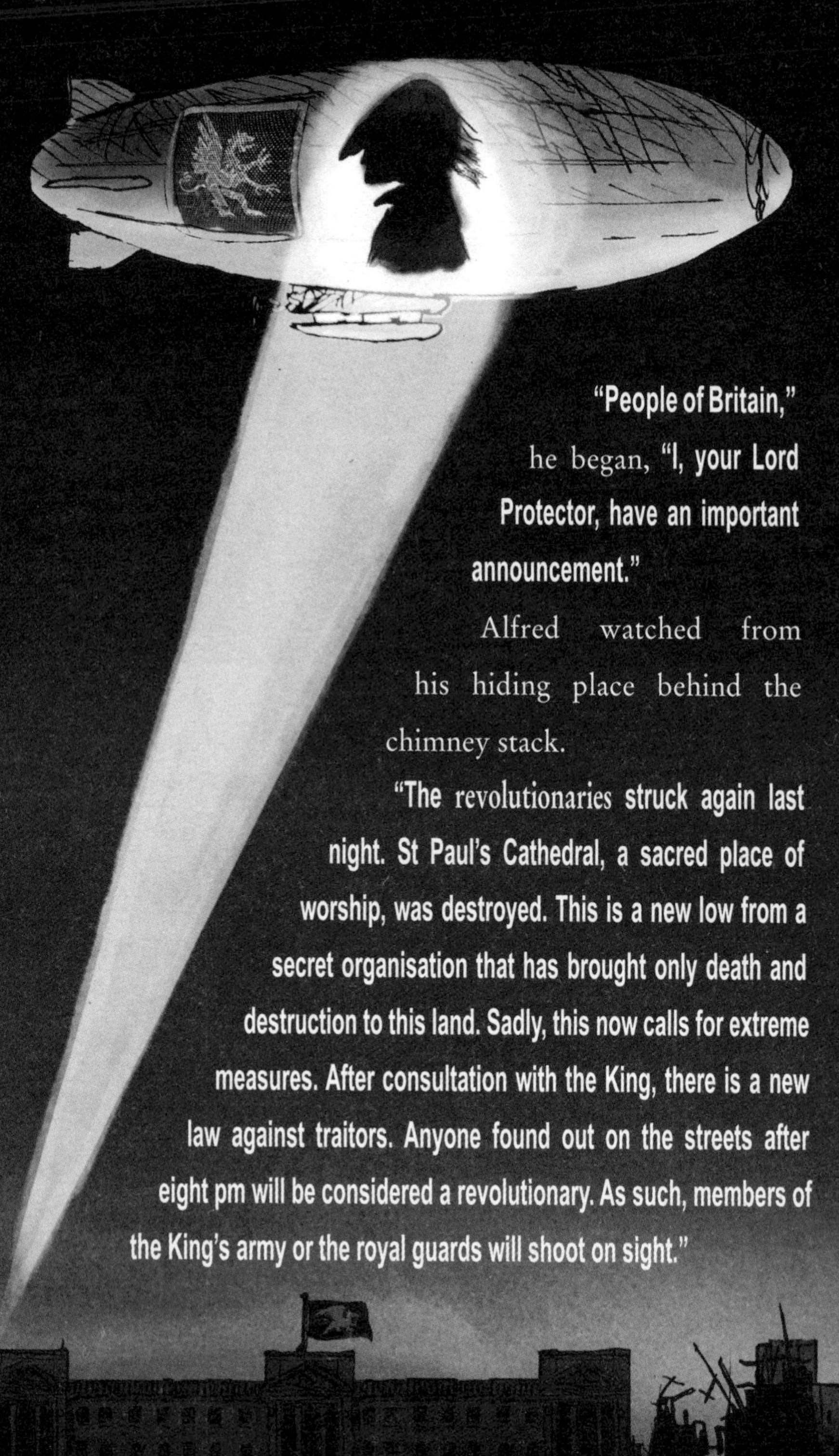

"People of Britain," he began, "I, your Lord Protector, have an important announcement."

Alfred watched from his hiding place behind the chimney stack.

"The revolutionaries struck again last night. St Paul's Cathedral, a sacred place of worship, was destroyed. This is a new low from a secret organisation that has brought only death and destruction to this land. Sadly, this now calls for extreme measures. After consultation with the King, there is a new law against traitors. Anyone found out on the streets after eight pm will be considered a revolutionary. As such, members of the King's army or the royal guards will shoot on sight."

Alfred shuddered. This was even more dangerous than he'd thought. He looked across the roofs of London towards Big Ben. The clock on the tower was about to strike eight.

"I wish you goodnight," ended the Lord Protector as his face flickered to black, and the airship disappeared back up into the clouds.

BONG!

BONG!

BONG!

BONG!

BONG!

BONG!

BONG!

BONG!

Eight o'clock. Alfred gulped.

GULP!

Might the royal guards shoot him on sight too?

Alfred scuttled across the palace roof. He found a small hatch, which he carefully opened and clambered through. Next, he dangled by his arms for a moment, before dropping down on to the carpet below.

THUD!

Now he was back inside the palace, and ***tonight's adventure could begin…***

CHAPTER 16

Spying Through a Keyhole

Buckingham Palace was eerie at the best of times, and especially at night.

Alfred made his way down the long, sweeping staircase, treading on each step lightly in case it made a sound. He patted his top pocket. The pad and pencil he needed for taking notes were still there. As Alfred drew nearer and nearer to the ballroom, he noticed there were some discordant sounds coming from it. So, when he reached the huge wooden door, he knelt down and peeped through a keyhole.

The entire room was illuminated by candles. They had been placed on the floor in some kind of formation, perhaps in the shape of a star. It was difficult to tell exactly.

Members of the royal guard stood to attention as the Lord Protector, with an old red leather-bound book in his hand for reference, was marking the floorboards with chalk.

So the Lord Protector was behind those strange markings! But what was he drawing or writing? And was that book the mysterious ***Book of Albion***?

When the Lord Protector had finished, the wooden

floor was covered in chalk markings.

Then he gestured to a group of guards who were standing in the corner of the ballroom. On cue, they lifted a tall stone statue from behind them and placed it on the exact spot carefully indicated by the Lord Protector.

Alfred immediately recognised it.

It was a statue of a beast.

Not just any beast.

A griffin.

Half lion and half eagle, the griffin was a symbol of divine power.

A power that is impossible to imagine.

A power over life and death.

A power to create or destroy the universe.

Alfred recognised that particular stone statue of the griffin. It had once sat on the front wall of Buckingham Palace. But, like many valuable artefacts, it had been moved to safety inside.

Next, the members of the royal guard took their positions around the ballroom, like figures on a chessboard. Then, on the Lord Protector's signal, they began to sing. Alfred tuned his ear in as much as he could. It wasn't a song exactly, more of a chant. The noise they made was unsettling, as if they were conjuring someone from the dead.

The Lord Protector began reading aloud from the book. He was speaking in some ancient language.

The sound of his voice and the chanting from the

royal guards grew louder and louder until a figure appeared through the tall double doors at the far end of the ballroom.

It was a man, bathed in the light of a thousand candles burning behind him. He was barefoot, wearing pyjamas.

From his long grey beard, Alfred immediately recognised the man.

It was his father,
the King...

CHAPTER 17

A Beast of Fire

The King looked as if he were sleepwalking as he moved straight towards the Lord Protector, stopping in the dead centre of the ballroom.

Alfred felt a pain in his heart. It was horrible seeing his own father look so lost.

The chanting grew louder and louder as the King held out his hand.

One of the royal guards passed the Lord Protector an ornate medieval sword. It had a distinctive jewelled handle, which glistened with all the colours of the rainbow. The man took the weapon, and slowly cut the King's hand.

SLICE!

Alfred winced from behind the door as he spied his father's blood trickle from his hand.

The Lord Protector then guided the King's hand until it was directly over the griffin.

DRIP!

DRIP!

DRIP!

The blood spilled on to the head of the statue.

Then, as if by magic, all the candles in the ballroom went out at once, and the room was plunged into darkness.

BLACK.

Out of the gloom something began to take shape. At first it was nothing more than a flame. Then the flames grew and grew as they licked higher and higher. The heat and light from the flames felt a hundred times hotter and brighter than a roaring fire.

The flames were gold.

Gold fire.

Alfred closed his eye behind the keyhole for fear of being blinded. But, as much as he couldn't look, he had to. He rubbed his eye before putting it back to the keyhole. The flames were taking shape. Taking the shape of a beast.

A winged beast.

A beast made of fire.

The most powerful beast in all the universe.

The griffin.

And it was *alive*.

PART TWO

Power over Life and Death

CHAPTER 18

The Mouth of Hell

Alfred couldn't believe his eyes. The Lord Protector had conjured this mythical beast to life.

The book.

The ancient markings on the floor.

The chanting.

The medieval sword.

The King's blood.

All of them played their part in these dark arts.

No wonder the King had become nothing but a walking shadow! He seemed to be just a pawn in the Lord Protector's wicked game.

From the other side of the keyhole, Alfred watched the scene unfold.

The griffin beat its mighty wings, and the golden

flames licked the walls of the palace ballroom. It was like looking into the mouth of Hell.

Death.

Destruction.

This was evil in its purest form.

All would be forced to kneel before it or suffer a terrible fate at the claws of this beast.

The griffin let out a deafening cry.

"WAAAAAK!"

The bombproof glass windows cracked.

CRACK!

Plaster fell from the ceiling.

RUMBLE! The sound was so loud that the King covered his ears in pain. All of a sudden, he came back into the land of the living.

"NOOOO!" he cried as he leaped at the Lord Protector to wrestle the ancient sword from his hands. "I won't do this! Set me free!"

The royal guards pounced on him, but he just managed to grab the sword and lunge at the beast.

"AAARGH!" he screamed as the sword sliced through the griffin's heart of fire.

WHOOSH!

In the blink of an eye, the mighty beast vanished.

Into air.

Into thin air.

It was as if it were nothing more than an illusion.

The King dropped the sword…

CLANK!

…as the Lord Protector's face darkened with fury. He gestured to one of the guards, who struck the King hard across the face with his gloved hand.

THWACK!

It knocked the King out cold. He collapsed to the floor with a THUD.

From behind the tall wooden door, Alfred desperately wanted to call out to his father, but he was frozen in fear. After all, he had just seen a monster.

Just as the boy was about to tiptoe back up to his bedroom, he felt someone or something looming behind him.

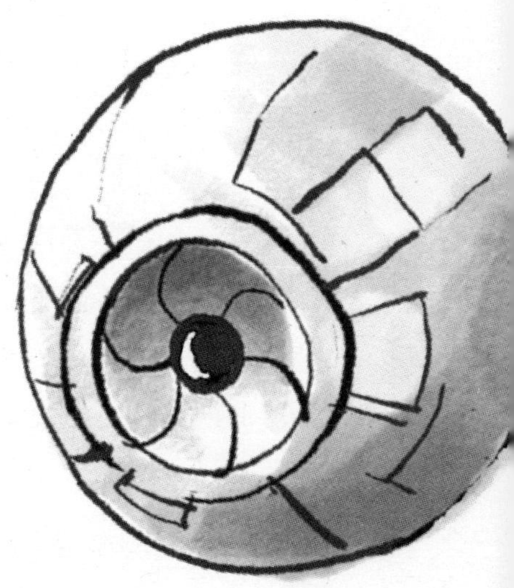

Slowly he turned round.

The All-Seeing Eye was staring right back at him.

They were eye to gigantic eye.

The game was up.

CHAPTER 19

Silent Scream

Alfred had been discovered out of his bedroom in the dead of night. He'd seen things he should never have seen. Goodness knows what the Lord Protector would do to him now – have him sent to the Tower of London or worse!

Alfred had to escape.

And *fast.*

"Goodbye!" chirped the boy as he dashed off down the corridor as fast as his little legs could carry him.

The All-Seeing Eye pursued him at speed.

As Alfred turned a corner, he tripped over the OCTOBUT, which was trundling along the floor.

CLUNK!

"OOF!"

The robot had been carrying a silver tray in one of its three remaining arms. On it was a pair of stinking old boots.

"Would you care for a crumpet?" asked the robot brightly, even though it was on its back, waggling its arms in the air like an upturned beetle.

With all his strength, Alfred righted the robot, and gave it back its tray. "That way!" he said, as he set it off in the direction from which he'd come.

As the All-Seeing Eye came whirring round the corner, the strangest thing happened. Something Alfred had never seen before. The flying robot's pupil opened, and a laser blast shot out.

ZAP!

BOOM!

It hit the poor OCTOBUT right on one of its three remaining arms.

CLANG!

It clunked to the floor. The arm with the iron in its hand was now detached. The OCTOBUT was down to two arms. A Bibut.

"I never did care much for ironing," commented the robot butler.

ZAP!

BOOM!

Another blast shot from the All-Seeing Eye. This one skimmed the top of Alfred's head, singeing his hair.

SIZZLE!

Was that a warning shot? Or was it meant to kill? Whichever, it was too close for comfort.

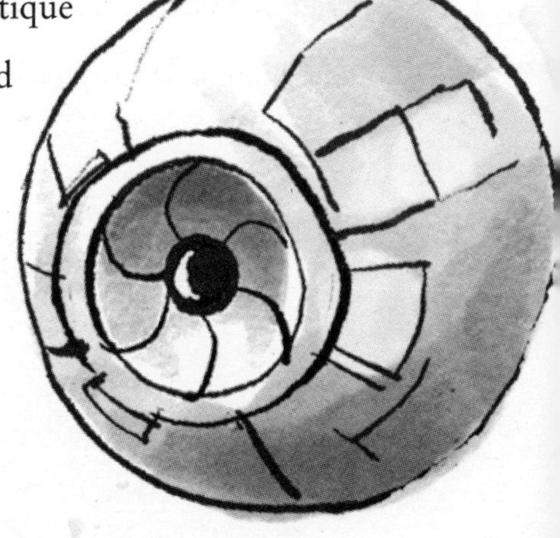

Alfred picked up the antique silver tray the OCTOBUT had been carrying and lifted it to his face, using it as a shield.

ZAP!

To Alfred's surprise the silver tray deflected the laser blast, and it shot right back at the All-Seeing Eye.

ZAP!

BOOM!

The flying robot blasted itself back down the corridor.

ZOOM!

WHOOMPH!

The boy couldn't help but smile as it hit the wall.

Alfred seized his chance to get away. With the tray still in his hand, he hurried further down the corridor. At the end, a long spiral staircase led down to the servants' quarters. He leaped on to the tray, and using it as a skateboard he sped down the stone steps.

CLUNK!
CLUNK!
CLUNK!

This was FUN!

Alfred looked over his shoulder.

NO!

The All-Seeing Eye was following close behind.

ZAP!

BOOM!

Another laser shot.

CLUNK! CLUNK! CLUNK!

ZAP!

BOOM!

And another.

CLUNK! CLUNK! CLUNK!

This time Alfred couldn't use the tray as a shield as he was standing on it! What's more, he was going way too fast to stop!

ZAP!

BOOM!

CLUNK! CLUNK! CLUNK!

Alfred threw his weight to one side, deliberately swerving the tray into the wall.

SMASH!

It scraped along the plasterwork, sending a cloud

of dust and debris into the air as the boy continued his descent.

WHOOMPH!

CLUNK! CLUNK! CLUNK!

The All-Seeing Eye raced straight into the cloud of dust. Losing sight of where it was headed, it bashed into the wall.

DONK!

It must have short-circuited. The life went out of it, and it began bouncing down the steps like a mighty bowling ball.

BOINK! BOINK! BOINK!

Alfred looked over his shoulder again.

CLUNK! CLUNK! CLUNK!

The ball was bounding straight towards him!

BOINK! BOINK! BOINK!

CLUNK! CLUNK! CLUNK!

As he reached the bottom step, he leaped off the tray and rolled to the side.

BOINK!

The All-Seeing Eye bounced down on to the tray,

sending it flying.

BOOM!

CLATTER!

The robot came to a stop further down the passage.

Alfred looked up from the floor. The thing was fizzling back to life.

FIZZLE!

Exhausted, the boy clambered to his feet.

With his mother in the Tower of London, Alfred had only one ally in the palace.

Nanny.

She was the only one who could help him right now.

Ahead of him was a little hatch in the wall, just big enough for a boy, but too small for a giant eye. It was a laundry chute, where all the sheets could slide down to the laundry room.

As the All-Seeing Eye rose off the ground, its deadly pupil swivelling round in his direction, Alfred had no choice. He ran for the laundry chute, and threw himself in.

WHIZZ!

He sped down the slide, landing in a big pile of dirty laundry collected in a huge wicker basket.

Alfred looked up from his comfy, if slightly smelly, bed.

There were rows and rows of sinks and washing machines. This was the laundry room all right. Knowing the All-Seeing Eye would still be looking for him, he leaped up from the pile of sheets and raced across to the door. Now he was in a corridor deep underground.

Alfred knew the servants' quarters were all the way down here, even if he'd never been. There was a strict division in the palace. The royals would never, ever venture down here.

The boy crept along the rows and rows of doors until he found the one he was sure was the right one. The door had the word **NANNY** engraved upon it.

Alfred lifted his hand, about to knock, before thinking better of it. It was far too dangerous to risk waking anyone else up. So, instead, he pushed down on the door handle.

LOCKED!

Just then, he heard the sound of boots stomping along the ground not far off.

STOMP! STOMP! STOMP!

It must be members of the royal guard on patrol.

Alfred bent down so his mouth was right next to the keyhole.

"*Nanny?*" he whispered through it.

Nothing.

"Nanny?" He was louder this time.

"Nanny?" Louder still.

Just as the bootsteps were growing closer and closer…

STOMP!

STOMP! STOMP!

…the key in the lock clicked.

CLICK!

A hand reached out from behind the door and smothered his mouth.

*Alfred wanted to **scream**, but*

***he couldn't let out** a sound!*

CHAPTER 20

Porridge & Port

The prince was hurled up and over…

"HUH!"

…and landed on his back, sprawled out on the floor.

THUD!

"OOF!"

A figure was standing over him in the blackness.

"What do you think you are doing out of your room at this time of night?" the voice demanded. "I thought you were locked in!"

"Nanny! You're surprisingly strong," said the boy as he lay there, dazed and confused.

The old lady proudly shared her fitness regime. "Porridge every morning and a bottle of port each night."

Indeed, the stench of alcohol coming from the old lady was overpowering. Alfred thought he might get drunk on the fumes.

"Would you like a hand up, Your Royal Highness?" asked the tough old bird.

"Yes, please."

With ease, the old lady yanked him to his feet.

"You won't believe what I've just seen," said Alfred.

Outside the door, the bootsteps were growing louder.

STOMP!

STOMP! STOMP!

"SHUSH!" shushed Nanny. "The guards will hear us. And we'll both be sent to the Tower!"

The pair waited until the sounds of the bootsteps

rose then fell, disappearing off down the corridor.

"Now you and I need to have a talk, young man." Nanny's tone was the one grown-ups use just before they tell you off.

"Let me tell you something first," pleaded Alfred. "It is super important!"

"No! No! Sit down, young man! Let *me* tell *you* something!"

"All right, all right, I'll sit down. But where?"

The problem was that it was pitch-black in Nanny's bedroom.

"Sit on my bed," said the old lady.

Alfred shuffled around the room with his arms out, attempting to feel his way to it.

"No, that's not the bed – that's a chest of drawers," hissed Nanny. "That's the coffee table. And what you're sitting on right now is me."

"Oh, sorry, Nanny."

Eventually, the boy found the bed and Nanny began her whispered tirade.

"You are going to get yourself killed, prince or

no prince, sneaking around the palace at night. It's dangerous."

"Have you finished?" asked Alfred.

"Don't you 'have you finished' me!" she hissed.

"Nanny! Please! You have to listen! I have to tell you something, something that you're not going to believe."

"I can believe a lot," mused the old lady.

"Trust me, you are *not* going to believe this!"

"Well, get on with it, then!"

"I am getting on with it!"

"Go on, then!"

"If you stop speaking, then I can!"

"I won't say another word," replied Nanny.

Alfred took a breath, and then began. "There is a beast in Buckingham Palace."

There was a pause before Nanny asked, incredulous, "A what?"

"A beast. A real-life griffin, just like on the flags and armbands!"

"A real-life one?"

"YES!"

"That's impossible," she scoffed.

"It's not impossible. I saw it with my own eyes!"

"Oh, *my little prince*, you just had a bad dream, you poor thing. A nightmare."

"This was no nightmare. This was real."

Nanny shook her head, and tutted. "Tut! Tut! Tut! What an imagination you have, young man! Let's get you back to bed right away. Come on. Chop chop!"

"NO!" replied Alfred firmly.

They sat in silence for a moment.

"I wish you wouldn't raise your voice like that, Your Royal Highness," began Nanny. "The guards will hear us."

"I'm sorry, Nanny," he whispered. "But, please, I beg you. I need you to believe me."

The old lady dismissed him again. "But it's not true, Alfred. A beast in Buckingham Palace! It can't be."

The boy thought for a moment before he replied. **"Then let me prove it to you."**

CHAPTER 21

The Vault

The next thing Nanny knew, Alfred was leading her out of her bedroom in the dead of night.

"Being out of our beds at this late hour with the palace teeming with guards – are you nuts?" she demanded as they tiptoed along the corridor of staff bedrooms.

The prince pondered this for a moment. "Probably a little bit, yes. It runs in the family. Always has!"

"Where on earth are you taking me?"

"I think I know where the statue of the griffin came from – the one they used to bring the beast to life. Come on!"

Alfred dragged the old lady along the corridor to a steep flight of ancient stone steps. He didn't dare turn on the lights. That would alert the royal guards, or, worse still, the deadly All-Seeing Eye. Instead, the pair lit two old lanterns that were left at the top of the stone steps to light their way down.

Slowly,

they descended

the steps

until they were in the

deepest

depths

of Buckingham Palace. They lifted their lanterns to reveal a vast cellar – so vast it spanned the entire length and width of the palace.

The vault.

It was bigger than a football pitch.

The vault was where all the countless gifts given to the royal family over hundreds of years were stored. Most of them were unwanted, but far too precious to throw away. There were thousands of wooden crates and boxes storing treasures, and plenty of *bizarre* items on display too.

AN AFRICAN TRIBAL MASK.

A harp that plucked itself.

A stuffed polar bear from the Arctic in mid-roar.

A samurai suit of armour complete with sword.

A model of an ancient warship.

A dozen ornate jewelled Fabergé eggs from Russia.

A giant marble throne from Ancient Rome.

A 500-piece gold tea set.

A death mask for an Ancient Egyptian pharaoh.

A bronze bust of some dictator or other, who had gone by the name of "Trump".

Since the kingdom had been plunged into darkness, many royal treasures had been moved down to the vault to keep them safe. **Priceless paintings, gold statues** and ANTIQUE FURNITURE were now stored amongst the many curiosities.

Alfred had been down to the vault many times before. It was the perfect place for a game of Hide and Seek. His mother used to bring him here when he was little, and together they had whiled away many a happy afternoon – him hiding, and her scooping him up in her arms when she found him.

On one of those afternoons, the pair had stumbled upon a number of **spooky stone statues**. They were statues of creatures.

The mightiest of them was the griffin.

On discovering the statues, the Queen had taught her son that these creatures were the **King's Beasts**: ten creatures that represented the British royal family through the ages. Intrigued, the boy then spent many an hour reading up on them.

"There should be ten stone statues down here somewhere," Alfred began.

"So?" asked Nanny.

"So one of them was used to bring the griffin to life."

"Oh, we're back to that, are we?" sighed the old lady, rolling her eyes.

"Yes! We are!"

"It's way past your bedtime."

"I don't care about boring bedtime!" snapped the boy. "We need to find them! Now!"

Nanny huffed and puffed. "Well, can you at least remember where they were? This place goes on forever."

Alfred lifted his lantern to take in the vast room. "Turn left at the **sphinx**..."

He began walking, with Nanny staying close behind. Their footsteps echoed in the darkness.

"Straight on to the **gold coffin,"** he continued as they walked. "Then a left. Then look out for the **bust of Medusa."**

Alfred placed his hand on the head of snakes.

"If I remember right, the beasts should be just ahead of us."

The boy lifted his lantern. Leaning out of the gloom were a number of stone statues.

The King's Beasts.

CHAPTER 22

The King's Beasts

"Now, a bit of a quiz for you, Alfred," began Nanny as the pair stood together in the middle of the vast vault at the bottom of Buckingham Palace. "Can you name all ten of the **King's Beasts?**"

Alfred sighed. The old lady could be annoying at the best of times, and this was the worst of times. She'd been working at the palace for so many years, over two generations, that she knew more than most about anything royal.

"Of course I can!" he protested. "I am Prince Alfred. One day I will be King. And they will be *my* beasts!"

"Go on, then," she replied, a know-it-all sing-song tone creeping into her voice.

Alfred sighed louder this time, then took a moment to gather his thoughts.

"Well, the Lion of England."

"Anyone can get that one," scoffed Nanny.

"The RED DRAGON OF WALES, the UNICORN OF SCOTLAND..."

"Those three are *easy-peasy lemon-squeezy*!"

"Nanny!" said the boy sharply. "You are actually distracting me by interrupting all the time."

"I won't say another thing," replied the old lady, looking unbearably smug.

"Thank you."

After a moment, she added, "Three. You've got three."

"That's you saying another thing!" he protested.

Nanny then performed the internationally recognised mime for zipping up your mouth. The boy continued, lighting up the statues one by one with his lantern to prompt him. They were all a good deal taller than he was.

"The **White Greyhound of Richmond**, the **White Horse of Hanover**, the **White Lion of Mortimer**, the **Black Bull of Clarence**, the Falcon of the Plantagenets..."

Nanny nodded her head, impressed, before pointing to the last stone statue in the line.

The prince took a closer look at this particular beast. It was the weirdest-looking creature of all, and he knew it had the weirdest name too. He shook his head. NO! He always forgot the last one!

"Can I give you a clue?" asked the old lady, grinning.

"NO!" he snapped.

"The Yale of Beaufort," she announced.

"That's not a clue!" exclaimed Alfred. "That's the actual answer!"

"Well, we haven't got all night."

Alfred counted them. "One, two, three, four, five, six, seven, eight, nine! Nine statues. **Nine.** There should be ten **King's Beasts!** One is missing. The one I said the Lord Protector was using!"

The boy felt vindicated.

Nanny swung her lantern around the vault and stopped when she spotted something.

"No, no, no," she said. "I am sorry, *my little prince*, but you are wrong. Quite wrong. It is right here!"

She lifted her lantern up to the statue.

"What?" He paced over to it.

Nanny was right. The stone statue of the griffin was standing there.

"The **Griffin of Edward the Third,**" she announced in a smugger-than-smug tone. "This great thing can't have been upstairs in the ballroom coming to life or some such nonsense, because it's been down here all along! Now! Can we please go back to bed?"

Alfred was stumped.

He knew what he'd just seen in the ballroom. If only Nanny would believe him.

"The guards must have brought it back down!" he protested.

"No, no, no," she replied. "We would have heard them. And look! These great blighters weigh a tonne!"

To prove her point she slapped the stone.

SLAP!

It was rock solid.

The old lady shook her head. "There is absolutely no way one could be carried all the way upstairs to the ballroom and all the way down here in so little time."

"How can you be so sure?" asked Alfred.

"It's just common sense, child."

Common sense was something Alfred knew he had precious little of, being a prince and all that.

The boy brought his lantern up close to the statue of the griffin. He noticed a dark patch on its head.

"Blood!" he exclaimed.

"You what?" replied Nanny.

"This was the statue the Lord Protector was using to bring the griffin to life. Look! There are spots of my father's blood on it!"

Nanny furrowed her brow before peering in for a closer look. She shook her head.

"That's not blood. That's just a dark patch on the stone!"

Alfred dabbed his finger on it.

"Then why is it still damp?" he asked, proudly showing her his stained red fingertip.

"It looks like dirt to me!" she muttered, dismissing him again.

The boy couldn't hide his frustration any more. "Why is everything 'no, no, no' with you?"

Nanny shook her head. "*My little prince*, you're tired. Overtired. You need to go to bed. Right now! If you really, really want to, we can look again in the morning. Once you've had your **eggy-wegg**, you will feel right as rain!"

"The morning may be too late! Who knows what the Lord Protector will have used his dark arts to do by then!"

"I've heard quite enough of this nonsense, young man! Come on, I am taking you up to bed. RIGHT NOW!"

With that, she grabbed the boy sharply by the wrist.

"OW!"

It hurt. In the struggle, he dropped his lantern on the floor.

CRASH!

The shock of this made the pair fall silent.

They listened, and to their horror heard a noise.

RUSTLE!

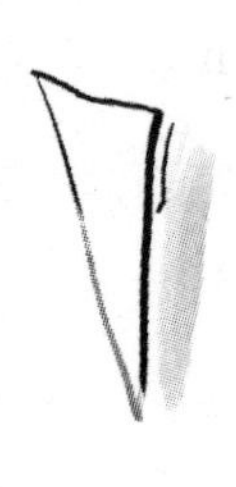

They were not alone down there.

CHAPTER 23

The Impossible

RUSTLE!

There was that noise again.

Alfred and Nanny didn't say another word. Instead, she dimmed the light on her lantern until the vault was all but black.

RUSTLE!

And again!

In a room as vast as the vault, it was impossible to work out exactly where a sound was coming from. Every step they took on the stone floor echoed down the rows and rows of boxes...

SHUNT! SHUNT! SHUNT!

...and bounced off the walls.

The sound could be coming from far away...

Or much closer than you think.

RUSTLE!

Again!

Nanny indicated with her eyes where she thought the noise might be coming from, and they tiptoed through the dark towards it.

Alfred's mind was racing. After what he had seen tonight, he was half expecting one of the terrifying treasures down here to come to life.

A golem.

An Egyptian mummy.

A Native American thunderbird.

An Ancient Greek Hydra, a nine-headed snake.

Vlad the Impaler, so called because he executed thousands of people by stake.

Emperor Caligula of Ancient Rome.

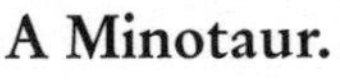

A Minotaur.

A Cyclops.

A Chinese dragon.

Or, worst of all,
the hound of Hell,
a three-headed dog.

Anything was possible. The impossible was possible. Alfred was shaking with fear.

RUSTLE!

There it was again.

Perhaps it is just a rat, he kept telling himself. But it sounded way too noisy to be a rat. *A giant rat?* he thought.

RUSTLE!

When he and Nanny thought they were near to the source of the sound, they stopped dead still.

RUSTLE!

Whatever it was, it was hiding on the other side of a huge leather trunk.

Alfred gulped.

GULP!

Nanny gulped.

GULP!

Nanny indicated for Alfred to have a look.

Alfred shook his head.

Alfred indicated for Nanny to have a look.

Nanny shook her head.

Nanny indicated for them to go together.

They both nodded their heads.

The pair held hands and tiptoed round the trunk to find…

CHAPTER 24

The Secret Passage

Mite!

"Hello?" she chirped from behind the leather trunk.

"It's you!" exclaimed Alfred, his voice echoing around the vault.

"Yep, it's me!" replied Mite. "And it's you, whoever you are!"

Her face was even dirtier than usual. She had a packet of something brown, no doubt swiped from the kitchen, that she was munching on. And she had got it all around her mouth.

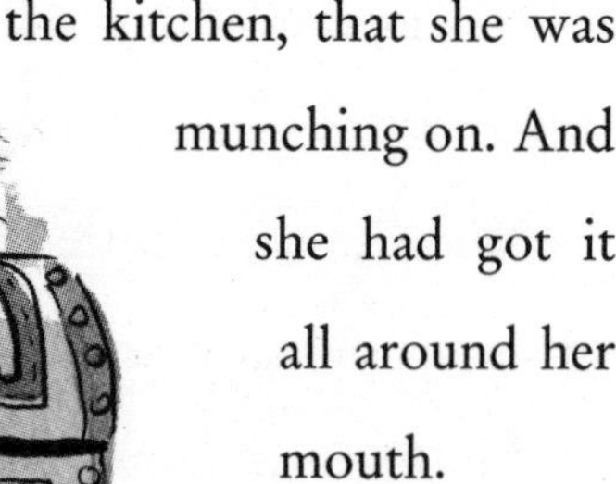

"What have you got there?" demanded Nanny.

"Chocolate!"

"Give me that!" ordered the old lady.

She went to snatch the packet, and a struggle began.

"NO!" protested the girl.

"Give me that!"

"I said 'no'!"

"LADIES, PLEASE!" ordered Alfred. "This is unseemly."

"You wot?" asked Mite.

It was enough of a distraction for Nanny to wrench the packet out of the girl's filthy little hands. She sniffed it.

"This isn't chocolate!" scoffed Nanny.

"Wot is it, then?" demanded Mite.

"Stock cubes."

"I did think they tasted a bit meaty. I never had chocolate before, so I dunno wot it tastes like, do I?"

With that, the little girl snatched the packet back from the old lady, and carried on munching.

"Eurgh!" exclaimed Alfred.

"Now last time up in the junk room you gave us the slip," began Nanny. "You need to tell me where this secret passage is right now!"

"You're a right bossy one, you are!" was the girl's verdict.

Alfred had to stifle a giggle. She was absolutely right.

"I said, *right now*!" said Nanny, not the least bit amused.

Mite munched some more on her stock cubes. "I'll think about it."

"What do you mean, you'll think about it?"

"I'll let you know when I've finished this!"

Nanny sighed and tried a different approach. "If you do as I say, I will show you where all the chocolate is hidden."

The girl was tempted. "You will?"

"Oh yes. The palace has mountains of the stuff. To last a hundred years. You can help yourself to as many chocolate bars as you can carry."

"I can carry a lot!"

"**Milk** chocolate, **dark** chocolate, **white** chocolate, **mint** chocolate, **orange** chocolate, **ruby** chocolate, **caramel** chocolate, fudge chocolate, **nutty** chocolate!"

"Now I want some too!" said Alfred.

"All right, all right, I'll show you!" said Mite.

"Clever girl!" replied Nanny.

"Chocolate first."

Nanny sighed. "The kitchen is all the way up those stairs, and I bet that underground passage is somewhere down here."

"You're right," said Mite. "Follow me!"

She galloped along the vault, as the other two trailed behind.

"I nearly got caught earlier. There were all these guards down here," remarked the girl. "Moving something around in the dark. You just missed them."

Alfred shot Nanny a look.

"I told you it was true!" he said.

"What's true?" asked Mite.

"It's a long story," replied Nanny, shutting down the conversation. "Not for your ears. Now where is this secret passage?"

"This way!" chirped the girl.

Right in the furthest corner of the vault was a loose stone in the floor.

"It's under here," said Mite, stamping the stone with her bare foot.

"Show me!" demanded Nanny.

The little girl huffed and slid the stone away.

CHONK!

Peering down into the gloom, all three could see a series of stone steps leading to what sounded like a river.

RUSH!

"Down there used to be part of the **LONDON UNDERGROUND?**" asked Alfred.

"Yeah. You can still make out some of the station

names at low tide. PICCADILLY CIRCUS. GREEN PARK. KNIGHTSBRIDGE."

"The Piccadilly Line!" exclaimed the prince.

"Well I never," said Nanny. "It must be another secret escape route built during World War Two. So secret that nobody knew of it. Good girl!"

"Now I want my chocolate!" Mite demanded.

"Of course. Of course. You will have so much chocolate you'll be sick as a dog!"

"YES!"

"Here. Let me take you!" said the old lady, putting the girl's hand in hers. "*My little prince?*"

"Yes," sighed the boy.

"Funny name!" giggled Mite.

"I know," he agreed.

"*My little prince,*" began Nanny again, "you need to go straight back to your room!"

"BUT—!"

"No buts! You need to go now."

"But I want some chocolate too!"

"He's not having the fudge one!" argued Mite.

"I will bring you up a bar, just as soon as I've taken care of this little one!" replied Nanny.

Together they made their way out of the vault.

CHAPTER 25

The Shadows

Keeping in the shadows, Alfred went on ahead, tiptoeing his way from the very bottom of Buckingham Palace to the very top. When he returned to his bedroom, he locked his door behind him, and hid the key under his pillow. Then he paced across the room to the window. Slowly, so as not to arouse any suspicion from the guards outside, he pulled back his curtains to peek out. At first his eyes were drawn to the fires that blazed every night all over London. There was always unrest, and it was worse at night. Not far from the palace, a Union Jack was raised on a lamppost to cheers.

"HOORAY!"

It must have been **revolutionaries!** Maybe Mite? Maybe his mother? Maybe they were all part of the same movement?

Within moments the Lord Protector's airship descended from the clouds, the golden griffin gleaming on its side. At the base of the cabin, a gun revolved and fired at the flag.

ZAP! ZAP! ZAP!

BOOM!

The Union Jack exploded into flames.

"Enjoying the view, Your Royal Highness?" came a voice from the shadows behind him.

The prince froze in fear. He turned round slowly to see the Lord Protector sitting in an armchair in a dark corner of the room. The man had been there all along. Alfred was trembling with fear.

"Well, I, er, just…"

"Just what, sir?" purred the Lord Protector.

"I haven't been out of my bedroom. I promise."

"Is that so?"

"Well, just the once. I had to pop out to use the bathroom."

"But you have a bathroom right there," said the Lord Protector. Only his piercing eyes were clearly visible in the gloom. They indicated the half-open door leading to the boy's private bathroom.

"I mean I went to get a glass of water."

The Lord Protector chuckled to himself. "Then where is said glass of water?"

"I drank it."

The man shook his head. "You forget that the All-Seeing Eye sees everything."

Alfred gulped.

GULP!

He had been busted.

"The question is, Prince Alfred, what *did* you see?"

"Nothing," lied the boy. He knew he'd said it too quickly to be believed.

"Now, come, come, child. We are all friends here."

"I am not your friend," retorted Alfred.

The Lord Protector raised an eyebrow. There was more spirit in this sickly child than he had thought.

"Tell me exactly what you saw," he pressed.

"NOTHING!" protested the prince.

The Lord Protector rose to his feet and stepped out of the shadows. With a smirk he took the key from under the boy's pillow and unlocked the door. On opening it, Alfred saw that the All-Seeing Eye was hovering just outside.

"Perhaps my friend here will help jog your memory," said the Lord Protector.

With that, the All-Seeing Eye floated silently into the room.

Alfred stood by the window as the thing approached. He backed away until he had nowhere else to go.

"Tell me what you saw," demanded the Lord Protector.

Now the giant eye was staring right into the boy's eyes. Its pupil opened. Was it going to blast Alfred to pieces?

"I know you are in league with Nanny," said the man.

"No, no," lied Alfred, "Nanny has nothing to do with this. I swear! She is innocent!"

"I'm not so sure. I will deal with her in good time."

"No, no. Not Nanny. Spare her! I beg you."

"Then tell me what you saw."

"I DEMAND TO SEE MY FATHER!" exclaimed Alfred. The prince was sure he had played his trump card here.

"The King is sick," replied the Lord Protector.

"You have made him sick!"

The Lord Protector kept his cool, but said, "That is a vicious lie. I am the King's most loyal servant."

"You are anything but!"

The man shook his head. "This can all be over right now if you just tell me what you saw."

"I demand to see my father!" Alfred repeated. He had the Lord Protector now.

"It is late. The King needs to sleep."

"Now!"

There was a pause before, to Alfred's surprise, the Lord Protector bowed his head, and said, "As you wish, Your Royal Highness."

With that, the Lord Protector made his way over to the huge gold-edged mirror on the bedroom wall. He pressed an unseen button on the side, and the image dulled to reveal the King standing on the other side of the glass, looking in from his bedroom. It was a two-way mirror.

"Father!" cried Alfred.

The All-Seeing Eye hovered to one side as the boy rushed to the mirror. He threw himself at the glass, embracing it.

However, the King just stared forward, not betraying a hint of emotion.

"Your son wanted to see you, sir," purred the Lord Protector.

Still the King said nothing.

"I regret to inform you that your son has been out of his bedroom tonight. We have reason to believe that, like his mother, the boy is in league with the **revolutionaries.**"

"THAT'S NOT TRUE!" protested Alfred. "FATHER! FATHER! PLEASE! YOU MUST BELIEVE ME!"

"What would you like me to do with him, sir?"

Alfred beat his fists on the glass.

BASH! BASH! BASH!

"FATHER! PLEASE! LISTEN TO ME! I BEG YOU!"

The King looked at his son. Alfred met his stare. He was desperate to see something in his eyes. Love. *Kindness.* **Pity.** Anything. But there was nothing. Nothing at all. Just a cold deathly stare.

"T-t-take the boy…" began the King.

"Yes?" encouraged the Lord Protector.

"T-t-take the boy to the Tower."

The Lord Protector smiled, and flicked the switch. In an instant, the King was gone.

"NOOOOOOO!"

screamed Alfred.

PART THREE

A TOWER OF TRAITORS

CHAPTER 26

Black Water

A hood was pulled over Alfred's head, so he couldn't see a thing.

Next, the condemned boy was marched along the corridors of Buckingham Palace by two royal guards, and down flights and flights of stairs. The Lord Protector led the way as the All-Seeing Eye hovered close behind. The guards held the boy's arms tight.

It was painful, and the prince could feel bruises blackening on his arms.

"Can I at least say goodbye to Nanny?" he pleaded, his voice muffled by the hood.

Maybe he could deliver a secret message to her.

Maybe she could save him.

"I am afraid not. Nanny is in the interrogation room as we speak. I expect her to be there for a long, long time."

The prince felt a pain in his heart. He desperately hoped he hadn't brought some terrible fate on the kind old lady.

"She is innocent!" protested the boy.

"We shall see. The interrogation is very –" the Lord Protector chose his words carefully – "persuasive."

"Torture!" exclaimed the boy.

"You'll find out for yourself soon enough."

Alfred began trembling so much he felt as if his legs were going to collapse beneath him. The guards took his weight, and began dragging him along.

A door opened and closed behind them. From the

unfamiliar sounds echoing around, Alfred guessed they were no longer in the palace.

TAP! TAP! TAP!

"Where are we?" he asked.

"If I told you, then it wouldn't be a secret."

It sounded like they were in some kind of narrow passageway.

"Where are you taking me?" demanded the boy.

"Be patient, young prince. All will be revealed!"

They walked some more before there was the sound of a very heavy door, or even wall, sliding to one side.

WHIRR!

Then there was the sound of it closing.

WHIRR!

The group took a few more steps forward, then finally came to a halt.

The guards held the boy still for a moment, before his hood was whipped off.

He blinked.

Prince Alfred was in the outside world for the very first time in his life.

Black water lapped at his feet and, looking up, he saw some stone arches. Instantly, he realised he was underneath a bridge.

Westminster Bridge, to be precise.

From his books on London, Alfred had learned that this bridge used to be one of the busiest in the city, with people and traffic continuously crossing the River Thames. Now Alfred could see that people had set up home all along the bridge in cardboard boxes and wooden crates. His heart ached for them as he noticed all they had over their heads to keep the rain out were old bits of tarpaulin.

Alfred looked behind him, but there was no entrance visible back into Buckingham Palace, just a stone wall. There must be some secret way in and out, but the Lord Protector was not sharing it.

"Your royal barge, sir," announced the man as the All-Seeing Eye hovered behind him.

Right on cue, a long wooden rowing boat, decorated with ornate carvings, painted mostly in gold, drifted into view. It was manned by at least a dozen royal guards, who lifted their oars as they reached the riverbank.

"Your Royal Highness, this is where I bid you

farewell," purred the Lord Protector. "For the very last time."

"You can't do this to me!" protested Alfred, struggling with the guards. "I'm a prince! I'm the heir to the throne!"

"You are nothing but a traitor. Guards! Take him to the Tower!"

As Alfred struggled…

"Get your hands off me! You are controlling my father, but you can't control me!"

…the guards gripped harder. Now they were squeezing his arms so tightly he was in agony.

"ARGH!"

"Is that so?" purred the Lord Protector. "Put him in chains."

Roughly, they led the boy down the slippery stone steps to the barge.

One metal chain went round the boy's feet, another round his hands, which were tied behind his back, and another acted as a collar round his neck. Then he was shackled to the flagpole at the front of the barge.

"I know what you're doing!" called out Alfred. "Creating some kind of **monster!**"

"It seems you are having visions, just like your father. The Tower should cure you of those."

The Lord Protector nodded, and the guards began rowing the prince away. The wooden oars sliced through the water in perfect time.

Swish! *Swash!* Swish! *Swash!* Swish! *Swash!*

On the riverbank, the Lord Protector, flanked by the All-Seeing Eye, gave the boy one final wave as the barge moved off.

"***Goodbye! Forever,***" he said.

Alfred turned his head away so the man wouldn't see his tears.

There was a thick fog over the River Thames, and the city seemed eerily quiet. Shapes and shadows unravelled themselves around the barge. Debris bobbed in the black water. Upturned boats, shoes, hats, books, suitcases, an umbrella, even a child's doll.

Each item told a story.

A horror story.

The boat swept along the Thames almost without a sound. The oars made much less noise than a motor, so the barge was perfect for transporting prisoners to the **Tower of London**. Alfred's thoughts turned to his mother.

This was the exact same journey she must have made.

From the bow of the barge, the boy could make out the shapes of London landmarks through the thick fog.

The London Eye, a huge wheel for people to travel on to see the sights, was now lying on its side. **The Globe**, a recreation of Shakespeare's theatre, lay in ruins. **Southwark Cathedral**, which had been without a roof since a fire had all but destroyed it, was now a blackened ruin.

As the barge approached London Bridge, Alfred could make out some figures standing amongst boxes and tents. The bridge, like the others along the Thames, was home to these poor souls. As the boat passed underneath, there were shouts and a barrage of sticks and stones hit the vessel.

BANG! BASH! BONK!

"WE NEED FOOD!"

"HELP US!"

"WE ARE STARVING!"

In desperation, some of the people leaped down from the bridge. A few missed the barge and fell into the water.

SPLASH!

When they tried to scramble aboard the boat, the guards whacked them away with their wooden oars.

THWACK!

They fell back into the river.

"DON'T!" screamed Alfred.

SPLOSH!

Two of them actually landed on the barge.

THUD!

THUD!

They came down at the stern and were immediately taken out with laser guns.

ZAP!

ZAP!

Their bodies plunged into the Thames.

SPLASH!

SPLOSH!

"MURDERERS!" shouted Alfred at the

royal guards, helpless to stop the horror.

The barge continued its journey along the Thames.

Slowly, out of the fog, an ancient building loomed into view.

The **Tower of London.**

At the base was its famous entrance from the river.

Traitors' Gate.

The prince closed his eyes. **He was about to meet his fate.**

CHAPTER 27

Traitors' Gate

All along the battlements of the **Tower of London**, Alfred could make out members of the fearsome royal guard. They had their laser guns pointed down at the river. As the royal barge approached the gate, it was raised.

CREAK!

Like so many traitors before him down the centuries, this was the way the boy was to begin his imprisonment in the Tower. With his hands and feet

still in chains, he was taken off the barge. Then he was bustled down a series of stone walkways until he reached the prison block.

Once inside, what hit Alfred first was the stench.

It was medieval.

Then the noise.

Constant cries of pain.

"ARGH!"

"HELP!"

"PLEASE!"

The Tower of London was the worst place Alfred could possibly imagine.

Prisoners were crammed into tiny cells – as many as a dozen to each dark, damp little space – and treated worse than animals in a zoo.

The prisoners' faces were blackened with dirt and hollow with hunger. They were dressed in rags with no shoes on their feet. When the boy was marched past the cells, some called out:

"Who's that boy?"

"Is it Prince Alfred?"

"What's he doing here?"

One toothless old lady just laughed and laughed in a way that made you think she must be mad.

"HA! HA! HA!"

A boy held out his hands to beg. "Please. Please."

Alfred wasn't sure what exactly he was begging for. Mercy, he supposed. Not that he could give it. The prince was now one of them, a prisoner too. He continued past his fellow inmates.

Was that old man in chains once commander of

the British Army? One night he had vanished from the palace.

Was the man with a long grey beard the old chief of police? He had not been seen in decades.

Was that Britain's last prime minister, shivering under a dirty old blanket? She had been arrested just before Alfred was born.

The Tower of London must have housed a hundred or more of these so-called "traitors".

The prince was desperate to catch sight of his mother. Was she even still alive?

As Alfred was dragged along the row of cells, he turned to the guards and said, "I am your prince and I demand to see the Queen."

But the guards just ignored him. Instead they tightened their grip on the prince's arms…

"OW!"

...and continued marching him to his cell.

Once there, the guards hurled the boy inside.

THUD!

"OOF!"

The chains round his arms and legs were unlocked...

CLINK!

...and the door was bolted behind him.

CLUNK!

Alfred ran to the rusty iron bars on the door of his cell and shouted at the guards.

"You can't just leave me here to rot!"

But they just had.

The prison cell hadn't changed much since the Tower of London had been built in the eleventh century. The walls were dark stone, hay was scattered across the floor, and in the corner crouched a little wooden bucket. Alfred presumed this was to do his business in. Being born a prince, Alfred had been sure he would be able to go through life without ever doing his business in a bucket. But he was wrong.

While Alfred felt that brief sense of bliss that comes with finally having a pee, he could hear a tapping on the ceiling.

TAP! TAP! TAP!

At first, the boy was irritated. This was really putting him off his pee.

But as soon as he'd finished he stood still so he could listen.

TAP! TAP! TAP!

Three in a row. The same rhythm as before.

TAP! TAP! TAP!

Alfred wanted to tap back, but even on his tiptoes

he wasn't tall enough to reach the ceiling. If only he hadn't filled that bucket with pee, he could stand on it.

TAP! TAP! TAP!

There it was again.

Oh, never mind! thought the boy. There was a tiny hole in the corner of the cell, down which he carefully poured the yellow liquid.

TRICKLE!

"Oi!" came a deep voice from below. "You dirty blighter!"

"Sorry!" he called back. He had only been in the Tower of London for five minutes, and he'd already upset one of the other prisoners by pouring pee on his head.

Next, Alfred overturned the bucket and stood on it. His hand just reached the ceiling. He clenched his fist and tapped back.

TAP! TAP! TAP!

Then, from above, there were another three taps.

TAP! TAP! TAP!

Alfred began to feel a little silly.

What on earth was the point of all this tapping?

Suddenly he heard scraping from above. Whoever was up there was trying to scratch a hole.

Alfred jumped down off the bucket, and on his hands and knees searched the floor of his cell. He was looking for anything sharp that could be used to dig from his side.

Nothing.

Out of the corner of his eye, he noticed that one of the stones in the wall was jutting out. Using the bucket, he smashed down on it…

BASH!

…chipping a bit off.

CHINK!

Then Alfred climbed back on the bucket and began scraping away at the ceiling.

SCRATCH!

SCRATCH! SCRATCH!

Outside he could hear bootsteps approaching.

STOMP! STOMP! STOMP!

A royal guard was on patrol!

Alfred leaped down and pretended to be going to the toilet by sitting on the bucket.

When a guard peered through the metal bars, the boy called back, "Do you mind? I used to be a prince, you know."

The guard shook his head and moved off.

Immediately, Alfred got back to work.

SCRATCH! SCRATCH! SCRATCH!

Eventually, grit fell down on to his face…

CRUNCH!

…as the hole was broken through.

Alfred put his eye up to it.

An eye stared back.

At first he was startled, until he realised he knew that eye better than his own.

It was his mother's.

CHAPTER 28

Sickness of the Mind

"Lionheart?" asked the voice from above.

Alfred wanted to be strong, but it was impossible. Immediately he burst into floods of tears.

"BOO HOO HOO!"

"SHUSH!" shushed the Queen through the hole in the ceiling of the cell. "The guards will hear you."

"I can't help it!" snorted Alfred.

"Don't be sad," she whispered.

"I'm not crying because I'm sad! I'm crying because I'm happy!"

"Happy?"

"Happy to see you!"

"Now you're going to make *me* cry," replied the boy's mother. "Here!"

The Queen pushed a lace handkerchief down through the hole.

Alfred took it and dried his eyes. Then he blew his nose.

HOO!

He studied the handkerchief for a moment, and read the letters sewn into one corner.

"VR. Victoria Regina! That's Queen Victoria. So this handkerchief is hundreds of years old."

"Yes. I shouldn't really be letting you snot into it."

"Sorry. Do you want it back?"

"That's awfully kind of you, but no."

"What should I do with it?"

"Pop it up your sleeve."

The boy did as he was told and pushed it into the sleeve of his pyjamas. The handkerchief felt all soggy next to his skin, and for a moment he wondered why grown-ups would ever do that.

"Mama, how I wish I could have one of your *special cuddles* right now."

"How I wish I could give you a *special cuddle.* I would give all my past, and all my future, to hold you in my arms right now."

"You're going to make me cry again," he sniffed.

"Alfred, let's have a *finger cuddle.*"

"A finger cuddle?"

"Yes! Here you go…"

With that, the Queen poked her finger down through the hole. Alfred stretched high on the bucket and poked his finger up.

They touched.

It felt strange and strangely comforting all at once.

"Why have you been sent here?" asked the Queen.

"Father sent me."

"No! How could he do that to his own son?"

"He's not well, Mama."

"You're right. There is an awful sickness in his mind. He would tell me about these terrifying nightmares. Night after night after night. Nightmares about some kind of fiery monster."

"They're not nightmares, Mama," replied Alfred. "They're real."

"What on earth do you mean?"

"You're not going to believe me, but I saw something in the palace during the night. Something truly horrifying."

"What?"

"The King was there."

"What was he doing?"

"It looked like he was sleepwalking."

"Sleepwalking?"

"Yes. Into this, well, I can't say exactly… ritual."

"Ritual? Was it just your father?"

"No, the Lord Protector was there."

"Of course! I should have guessed he would be behind it!" exclaimed Mother.

"Yes, using some dark arts, the Lord Protector was... He was..."

"He was what?"

The boy felt strange saying it, but he knew what he had seen. "Conjuring a creature to life."

"What kind of creature?"

"A creature made of fire! ***A griffin!***"

"A griffin," pondered his mother. "The symbol of divine power dating back thousands of years. Are you sure you weren't just reading one of your old books and then having a nightmare?"

"No," replied Alfred calmly. "This was real."

"Then this griffin must give the Lord Protector power over the King. The visions must have scared him half to death. Poor, poor man."

"But it isn't just a vision, Mama. And, if we don't stop it, **this beast will kill us all!"**

CHAPTER 29

Deception

Just then a bell tolled across London.

BONG!

It was the unmistakable sound of Big Ben.

"Count!" hissed the Queen through the hole in her floor and Alfred's ceiling.

Alfred listened as the bongs continued.

"...Two, three, four, five, six, seven, eight, nine, ten, eleven, twelve," he whispered.

"Not tonight, then," said his mother.

"What isn't tonight?" he asked, intrigued.

"We have to listen out for thirteen bongs."

"Thirteen? Why would there be thirteen?" asked Alfred, not unreasonably.

"That's the signal."

"For what?"

"Revolution!"

The boy couldn't believe his ears. The Queen was a traitor after all!

"So, you *are* a revolutionary!" spluttered Alfred.

"Yes," she replied calmly.

"But destroying St Paul's Cathedral! How could you?"

"That wasn't me!" protested the Queen.

"I don't understand."

"Please! You must believe me! I would never, ever do such a thing. And neither would the **revolutionaries**."

"How can you be so sure?"

"There is no reason for them to attack their own city. All they want, and I want, all the people of this country want, is an end to this evil rule."

"But if you or the other **revolutionaries** didn't destroy St Paul's Cathedral, then who did?"

"The Lord Protector," she replied coolly.

"But why would he do that?" asked Alfred. "It doesn't make sense."

"It makes perfect sense."

"To destroy St Paul's Cathedral?"

"No one would ever suspect the Lord Protector of doing that himself. Instead he could put the blame on the **revolutionaries**. On me. Frame us as the evil ones, and not him. And with me locked up here in the Tower, the Lord Protector has free rein of the palace so he can carry out his wicked plans! He is an evil dictator, and he must be stopped. Alfred, will you help us?"

Before the boy could answer, he heard the sound of bootsteps approaching.

STOMP! STOMP! STOMP!

"Guards!" he hissed.

"Go! Go! Go!" implored Mother, so he jumped down from the bucket, and leaped on to a pile of hay.

THUD!

There he pretended to be asleep. Alfred even did his best snore, though, as far as he knew, he didn't snore in real life.

"ZZZ!

ZZZZ!

ZZZZZ!"

The boy didn't dare open his eyes. He could hear the guard stop at his cell, and then move off.

STOMP! STOMP! STOMP!

He opened his eyes again, and heard voices from his mother's cell above.

"How dare you barge in here like this!" said the Queen.

"Tell us where your friends the revolutionaries are hiding!" demanded someone with a deep gravelly voice.

"I don't know!"

"Answer the question!" he barked.

"I swear I don't know," she replied.

"Come now, let's not play games."

"I command you, as your Queen, to release me from this godforsaken place. Oh! The noise! The people! You must set me free at once and let me return to the palace."

"Orders of the King himself," came the barked reply.

"The King is not well enough to give orders! I know him better than anyone! Please!"

The man was having none of it. "Orders of the King. All traitors are to be imprisoned in the Tower."

"I am not a traitor!"

"Oh yes you are. And you know where the revolutionaries are hiding. Tell us, and we can wipe out the traitor scum once and for all."

"For the last time, I don't know!" exclaimed the Queen.

"Then this calls for extreme measures," said the deep voice.

"Torture me again if you like! I still won't know anything!"

There was a long, low laugh.

"HUH! HUH! HUH! Oh no, we are not going to torture you. I have a much better idea about who we can make suffer. When you hear their screams, you will be sure to tell us everything you know!"

"WHO?" demanded the Queen. "TELL ME WHO, YOU BRUTE!"

"Your *son*, of course."

CHAPTER 30

The Executioner

Moments later, the boy was dragged kicking and screaming from his cell by two royal guards. They hauled him to one of the turrets on top of the Tower of London.

Thunderclouds rolled overhead as a wicked wind whipped through the sky. There, on the turret, was the Queen, squashed into a metal cage that was swinging in the air.

CREAK! CREAK! CREAK!

The cage was something that had been around since medieval times. It was used for "coffin torture". The cage was just big enough for the Queen's body, but not big enough for her to move. The expression on her face betrayed the agony she was in.

"MAMA!" cried Alfred upon seeing her.

"DON'T YOU DARE HURT MY SON!" yelled the Queen at the guards.

They threw the boy to his knees. He scrabbled up, and raced over to his mother.

He hurled himself at the cage, his little fingers poking through, desperate to comfort her.

"Be strong, *Lionheart*," she whispered. "Be strong. We're going to get out of here alive. I promise you."

Before the boy could reply, a giant of a man, his face hidden by a black hood, dragged him away.

He was the Executioner.

"YOU ARE COMING WITH ME, LITTLE ONE!" he said in his deep, rough voice.

This was the same man who had been interrogating the Queen in her cell not long before.

"NOOO!" cried Alfred.

But the Executioner was so much stronger than him. Soon the boy was tied to a huge wooden wheel.

Yet this wasn't just any wheel.

This was a Breaking Wheel, another instrument of

medieval torture: a giant wheel that revolved a person as their limbs were broken. One by one.

Without a word, the Executioner ensured that Alfred had been secured properly by yanking on the ropes round his ankles and wrists.

"ARGH!" exclaimed the boy as his skin was burned by the ropes.

However, the torture was yet to begin.

"Revolve the wheel!" called out the Executioner, and the royal guards did his bidding.

Slowly, Alfred began **turning** on the wheel. He felt **dizzy** as he hung all the way **upside down**. As the wheel revolved, he started to feel sick.

"Now, Your Majestical Majesty! Tell us where the **revolutionaries** are hiding," began the Executioner, "or your darling little boy will be crushed to death!"

"For the last time, I don't know what you're talking about!" shouted the Queen. "I would tell you if I knew anything, I promise. But I don't. Put me on that thing if you must. Not him. I beg you. He is just a child!"

"I wonder if when one of your son's limbs is smashed to pieces it might just jog your memory."

"NO! PLEASE!" she pleaded. "I DON'T KNOW ANYTHING. I SWEAR!"

The Executioner shook his head, before holding aloft an iron hammer, ready to strike the boy, and smash his bones into smithereens.

Alfred shut his eyes tight. He couldn't bear to watch what was about to happen to him.

"STOP!" called out the Queen. "I will tell you everything I know."

"I knew you'd see sense," replied the Executioner.

"Now, untie my son, and I will talk."

The Executioner was not used to taking orders. The man bristled and paced over to the cage.

"Where are the **revolutionaries** hiding?" he demanded.

"I said, *untie my son* first," said the Queen sternly.

Alfred was amazed that his mother could retain her composure at a time like this.

The Executioner nodded to the guards, who began loosening the ropes round the boy's wrists and ankles.

"Don't tell them anything, Mama," pleaded Alfred.

The Queen chose to ignore her son. She waited for him to be freed from the Breaking Wheel. The boy's eyes were streaming, and he was completely out of breath. He had to be helped up by one of the royal guards.

"Your *precious little prince* is free," began the Executioner. "Now you tell me what you know. Right. Now."

The man swung the head of the hammer into the palm of his hand.

THWACK!

A tiny bit too hard.

He had hurt himself.

"Ouch," he said, no doubt wincing underneath that hood. "I am waiting."

Next, he dragged the end of the hammer slowly down the bars of the cage.

CLUNK! CLANK! CLINK!

"Please. I am a very busy man. I have a whole tower full of prisoners to torture, and a list of executions as long as your arm!"

The Queen stared straight at Alfred and nodded her head. He struggled to understand what she meant. Without giving the game away, he furrowed his brow as if to ask, *What?*

The Queen nodded her head again, tilting it to one side.

This, the prince thought, must mean she wanted him to get the Executioner's attention.

"I will tell you where the **revolutionaries** are," announced Alfred. The Executioner turned round.

The Queen smiled. Her plan was working.

"Will you now, you nasty little wretch?" asked the Executioner, not sounding at all convinced. "Or are you just playing games?"

With all eyes on the prince, the Queen was free to rock her cage to and fro. In a few swings, the cage was gathering momentum.

WHOOSH!

Alfred did his best to let his face portray absolutely nothing of this at all. Which was hard, as it wasn't

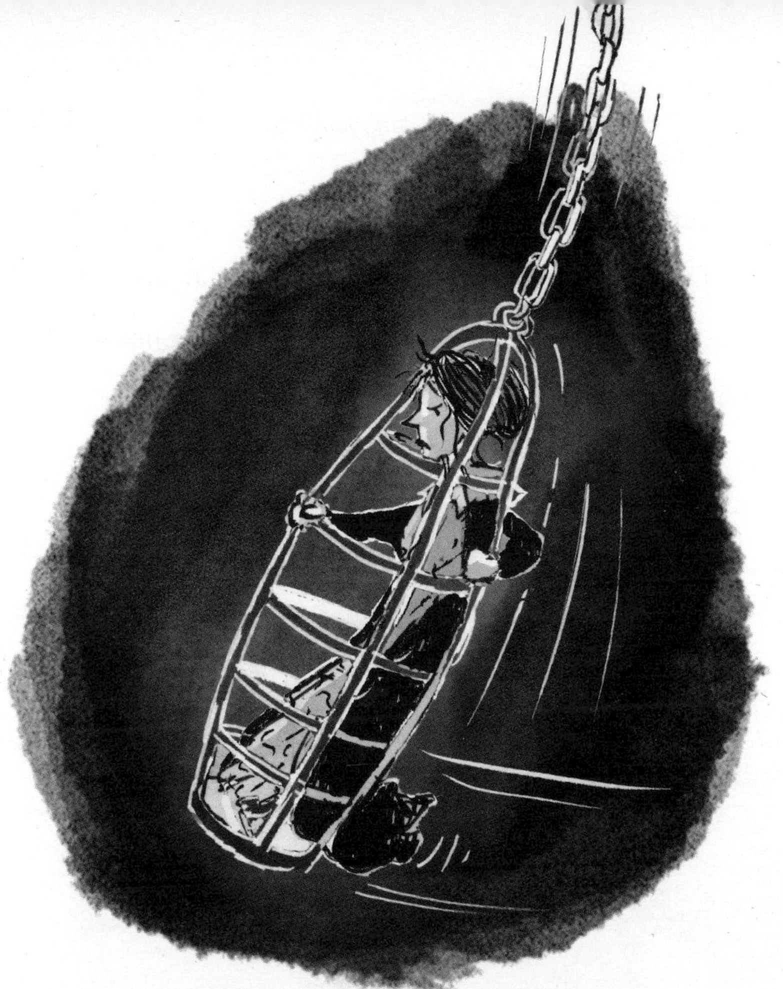

every day that he saw his mother swinging around in what looked like a giant birdcage.

"The **revolutionaries** have a number of secret bases across London," continued Alfred. "They hide in what used to be the **Underground** stations."

The Executioner rolled his eyes. "That is old information, and you well know it. The rats were driven out of those sewers years ago."

Now the cage was **swinging** violently. So violently, in fact, that it was very nearly reaching the Executioner.

"Executioner!" called out the Queen.

He turned round. "What?"

Only to be **whacked** on the head by the cage.

CLONK!

"OOF!"

He toppled over and fell off the top of the tower...

"ARGH!"

...plunging into the river below.

SPLOSH!

"I CAN'T SWIM!" he cried.

CHAPTER 31

Disaster Strikes

Standing on one of the turrets of the Tower of London, Alfred looked over to his mother for the next part of the plan.

Sadly, she didn't seem to have one.

"RUN!" she shouted.

"But, Mama, I have to save you!"

"RUN! PLEASE RUN!"

The boy looked across the turret. Guards were blocking the way down.

What's more, one of them was coming straight for him. Alfred escaped by darting round the back of the cage.

"WHACK HIM!" called out his mother.

With all his might, he swung the cage forward and

it smashed straight into the guard.

CLONK!

"EURGH!"

The guard toppled backwards, knocking over a few more guards, as if they were skittles.

"AH!"

"OW!"

"HURGH!"

"Nice work, young prince," said his mother.

The guards scrambled to their feet and were now circling Alfred.

"RUN, LIONHEART, RUN!" shouted the Queen. "Only you can save the kingdom now."

"NO! I'm not leaving you!"

With that, the boy leaped on to the back of the cage to make it swing faster.

BASH!

It smashed into one of the guards.

"Four down! One to go!" said Alfred.

"Don't get cocky!" remarked his mother.

However, Alfred didn't listen. He began swinging the cage as fast as he could. To create more momentum, he arched his back to go faster and faster.

As he did so, DISASTER STRUCK! Just as it swung off to the side, his hands slipped from the bars of the cage!

"ARGH!"

Alfred found himself falling through the air, heading straight for the River Thames!

"AAARGHHH!"

PART FOUR

REVOLUTION

CHAPTER 32

Some Kind of Monster

SPLASH! Alfred plunged deep into the black water.

He had dropped from so high that the force of the fall took him down and **down** and **down** into the depths. It was so **dark** and **cold** and **dirty** that he didn't know if he were upside down or the right way up. Gasping for air, he desperately tried to propel himself to the surface to take a breath. But, as much as he tried, he couldn't. Instead Alfred felt himself being swept along by a powerful current. His body was being twisted and turned by the flow of the water.

THUD!

Alfred's head had bashed into what felt like a brick wall. It must have been one of the legs of Tower Bridge. As much as he was dazed and confused, he knew that the bridge was the only thing that could save him. The water was pinning him to it. He grabbed on to the bricks with his hands. They were slippery and thick with slime, but the boy just managed to haul himself up.

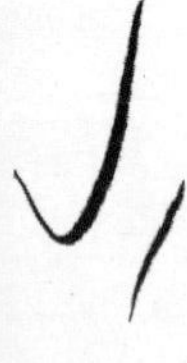

GASP!

He took a breath. He was alive. But not for long.

Not if those royal guards shooting at him with their laser guns were anything to go by.

ZAP!

ZAP!

ZAP!

The bricks just above his head exploded.

BOOM!

BOOM!

BOOM!

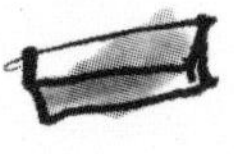

With his feet, Alfred pushed himself away from the wall and swam for his life.

The boy was coughing and spluttering, having taken in several mouthfuls of the filthy river water. It was years since any fish had lived in the Thames. It had returned to being little more than a giant sewer for the City of London, as it had been hundreds of years ago.

Hearing something surging through the water, Alfred turned round to see that the royal barge was giving chase.

As fast as the boy could swim, the boat could go faster.

There was only one thing for it.

GASP!

Alfred took a deep breath.

Then he swam down, down, down into the depths of the Thames until his ears went POP!

With his hands, he searched the muddy bottom for something, anything, to hold on to. The riverbed was a graveyard of wrecks. Old cars, sunken boats, even train carriages often poked out of the water at low tide. Finding a long piece of metal, he yanked himself down, and passed through what felt like a window. On the other side of the opening Alfred saw there was an air bubble just above him.

GASP!

He took a breath.

Feeling his way around, Alfred realised that there were rows and rows of seats. He couldn't believe it! He was on the top deck of a double-decker bus!

One of London's famous modes of transport, the once bright-red bus must have plunged off Tower Bridge many years before. Now it was an underwater hiding place for a prince.

The boy took slow deep breaths, counting in his head.

ONE...
TWO...
THREE...

He counted all the way to two hundred. Only then

could he be sure that the guards on the royal barge would have presumed him drowned and moved off.

By now the oxygen in the bubble of air was thinning. Alfred took one last breath…

GASP!

…before pulling himself out of the bus and letting himself float to the surface.

GASP!

He was alive!

His head bobbing out of the river, Alfred looked all around. There was now no sign of the royal barge, and the boy felt safe enough to swim again. However, the freezing-cold water was tiring him quickly. He had little energy at the best of times, and this was the worst of times. His arms and legs felt like lead weights, and in seconds he found himself whooshing downriver. The tide was taking him, and if Alfred didn't do something fast he would be swept all the way out to sea!

At speed, he passed through what was left of the Thames Barrier, like giant clogs in the water. It had been designed and built nearly two hundred years before to prevent a flood. Many years later, the barrier had been destroyed by one. Now it was little more than a mangled mess of metal, rusting in the water. Alfred tried to cling on to part of it, but the tide was so strong it pulled him off.

"NOOO!" the boy cried.

As Alfred was taken further and further downriver, he felt something move past him under the water. It was something fast and silent. At first, he thought it might be a whale or even a shark, but that was impossible.

Could it be some kind of monster?

Alfred was panicking and kicking his legs as hard as he could to escape from whatever was powering through the depths.

However, this thing was gaining on him.

WHOOSH!

What's more, it was rising to the surface.

WHAASH!

Alfred could feel the water around him being swept aside. Whatever it was, it was right underneath him.

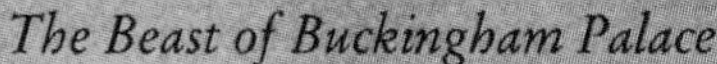

And it was rising fast!

The boy couldn't bear it and closed his eyes.

He was about to be eaten alive!

CHAPTER 33

HMS *Sceptre*

The prince lifted his hand as high into the air as he could. Maybe, just maybe, if he struck this creature hard enough, it might descend into the murky depths forever.

THWACK!

"OUCH!" cried Alfred.

This monster was made of metal.

As it emerged from the water, Alfred realised it wasn't a monster at all.

It was a submarine.

He was lying right on top of a submarine!

It looked like a relic from World War One, a rusty old antique that Alfred was surprised was still operational. On the front of the craft was emblazoned **HMS *SCEPTRE***.

Sceptre!

That was the code word he'd heard on the radio.

Revolutionaries!

Near the name was a painted Union Jack.

A hatch on the submarine opened, and to Alfred's surprise an elderly lady popped her head out. She was tall and proud, and dressed in a way that suggested she was making the best of things: a hat, a string of pearls and white gloves that had gone grey.

"The captain requests you come aboard, Your Royal Highness," she announced in a posh voice.

Alfred rose to his feet. Soaked to the skin and shivering with cold, he trudged over to the hatch.

"Ladies first!" he said.

"Very kind, but, please, after you, Prince Alfred," said the old lady, beckoning for him to make his way down the ladder. For the first time in his life, the prince was standing in a submarine.

"SUBMERGE!" barked someone from the shadows, and all at once half a dozen elderly ladies set to work. All Alfred could do was stand still as they bustled around him. Despite their age and in many cases infirmity (Alfred spotted some hearing aids, a walking frame and even a wheelchair), in seconds the submarine was sinking into the depths of the Thames.

"My goodness, you must be little Alfred," said the voice.

"Less of the little, please," he replied. "I'm now twelve years old."

"I haven't seen you since you were a toddler."

Then the owner of the voice stepped into the light and Alfred recognised her at once.

"GRAMMY!" he exclaimed.

"The very same!" she replied brightly. She held out her arms, and he raced towards her. It felt so good being held again by someone who loved him.

The King's mother had mysteriously disappeared from Buckingham Palace half a dozen years before. She was dressed in that way old queens often are: all in one colour. Today it was *canary yellow*, with a matching hat, handbag and long white gloves. Just like the lady who had welcomed him aboard, her clothes had seen better days. Living on an old, oily, dusty submarine couldn't help.

Grammy was a good deal older than Alfred remembered. She was stooped, and her skin was pale and wrinkled, though she still had that *magical twinkle* in her eye that made you fall in love with her in a heartbeat.

"You are wet through!" she remarked.

"I was swimming, Grammy," he replied.

"And you used to be such a sickly child! Well I never. Still, it's a ruddy stupid thing to swim in that dirty old river."

"I had to escape!"

"Yes. We've been spying on the Tower of London for some time now. We saw a figure dive from the very top. Must have been you. Extremely brave, I must say."

Alfred didn't tell his grandmother that it was not a dive at all, but rather a fall.

"Thank you, Grammy," he replied. "What are you all doing on board this submarine?"

The Old Queen smiled. "We're waiting for the right moment to **strike!**"

Surely they couldn't be?

Could they?

"Don't tell me that YOU are the **revolutionaries?**" he spluttered.

"YES! You are looking at them. I know we look like a group of *nice old dears* ready to judge a cake competition."

Alfred did not disagree.

"But," the Old Queen continued, "we are ready for **REVOLUTION!**"

All the ladies stood to face the prince and saluted.

"Are there any others?" asked the boy.

"Of course! We are just one group," continued Grammy. "One group of many."

"But you are a member of the royal family!" exclaimed the boy. "How can you be a revolutionary too?"

"What binds all us **revolutionaries** together is an idea. An idea that the way this once-great nation is being run is wrong. There must be a better way. A fairer way. We need a government. We need a police force. We need food and water for everyone, whoever they are. Power can never lie in the hands of just one man. Especially if that man is the Lord Protector."

"So how many **revolutionaries** are there?" asked Alfred.

"Impossible to say. The Lord Protector and his goons have done their best to crush all of us. We hid in Knightsbridge Underground station for many years..."

"Very handy for looting Harrods," chirped one of the old ladies.

"But like many of the other **revolutionaries** we were driven out of our hiding place."

"How?" asked Alfred.

"The royal guards pumped poison gas down into the tunnels. We were lucky to get out alive. Some of our friends weren't so lucky."

The old lady's eyes glinted with tears at the memory. Alfred put his arm round his grandmother to comfort her.

"I've missed you so much, Grammy. I wished you hadn't left the palace," he said softly.

"I am sorry, Alfred, but I had no choice. The Lord Protector accused me of being a traitor. I was only a traitor to him, never to my son the King. My ladies-in-waiting and I escaped by a bit of ram-raiding!"

"What?"

"We all piled into an old Rolls-Royce and smashed through the palace gates!"

"Jolly good fun it was too!" added one of the others.

"Rather!" said another.

"I haven't introduced you properly!" exclaimed Grammy. "You will have seen these ladies bustling around the palace, but you were just a baby. This is Enid!"

"Good day!" trilled Enid.

"Agatha!"

"A pleasure," said Agatha, performing a curtsey.

"Virginia!"

Virginia did a little wave from her wheelchair.

"Daphne!"

"Charmed to meet you."

"Beatrix!"

"Or 'Beatie' for short!"

"Judith!"

"What?" said the old lady.

"I'm introducing you!"

"Pardon?"

"Judith is a little deaf."

"Half past two."

Alfred smiled to himself. "So how did you come to be on this submarine?"

"We stole, I mean 'borrowed', the *Sceptre* from the naval museum. Ancient old thing she is, a little like me!"

"Ha! Ha!" chuckled Alfred.

"Now, Alfred, we need you to share with us all the intelligence you have from the palace."

The boy was worried he was going to be laughed at. "You are not going to believe this..."

"These days, there is nothing that can surprise me," replied Grammy.

Alfred took a deep breath before blurting out, "There is a beast in Buckingham Palace. A griffin. Made of fire."

There followed a pause long enough to sail a warship through it.

"I have to be honest, that has surprised me," replied the Old Queen.

"I knew you wouldn't believe me!" protested Alfred.

"What do you mean 'a griffin made of fire'? Griffins are the stuff of myth and legend! They are not real!"

"No, this one is real, Grammy. I promise you. The Lord Protector has used some dark arts to bring a stone statue of a griffin to life. If we don't stop him, this beast will kill every last one of us."

The old lady pondered this for a moment. She took out a long, thin white thing from her handbag.

"What's that?" asked the boy.

"A cigarette."

Grammy put the cigarette in an elegant black holder, which she placed between her teeth. Then she found some matches and lit the end.

STRIKE!

Instantly, foul-smelling smoke clouded the air.

"What on earth are you doing, Grammy?" spluttered Alfred between coughs.

"Smoking..." She took a long, deep drag. "Something foolish folk like me used to do in the olden days. Something that you must ***never, ever*** do."

The boy shook his head. Grown-ups were weird. This was a disgusting habit.

Next, the old lady brought out a little silver container, called a hip flask, and took a swig.

"What's in there?" asked Alfred.

"Gin! Yes! I am drinking alcohol. Another thing you must ***never, ever*** do."

"Anything else while you're at it?" asked the boy.

The Old Queen took another drag on her cigarette, before enjoying another swig of gin.

"Gambling. Swearing. Cheating at cards. Putting ten sugar lumps in your tea. Eating toast in bed. Picking your nose. Peeing in the bath. Blowing off and blaming it on someone else. Scratching your bottom in public. All horrible habits that you must promise to ***never, ever*** do."

Alfred couldn't help but smile when he replied, *"I promise, Grammy."*

"Good boy. Now if what you say about this beast is true..."

"It is true."

"...then this Lord Protector is more powerful than we had ever imagined."

The Old Queen took the cigarette holder out of her mouth and hollered, "LADIES!"

The old dears gathered around their mistress.

"We must stop the Lord Protector in his evil plan! We will strike... tonight!"

"TONIGHT?" spluttered Enid.

"Yes. Tonight! We will sound the signal for the people of Britain to rise up against this tyranny!"

"Thirteen bongs of Big Ben!" said Alfred.

"So you are one of us!" replied Grammy. "We will make a revolutionary of you yet! Set sail for the Houses of Parliament!"

"But, Your Majesty," began Agatha, the rotund lady with the walking stick, "the Houses of Parliament are still under the control of the royal guards. The intelligence tells us they have doubled their soldiers there. To break into the bell tower now would be suicide."

Grammy took another long drag on her cigarette.

"Then, Agatha, I, the Old Queen, will lead the attack."

Silence descended upon the submarine.

"Grammy, with respect, you are too old to take on such a dangerous mission!" protested Alfred.

"You are never too old for adventure!" she retorted.

There was a hurrah from the ladies on board.

"HURRAH!"

Looking around, Alfred realised that his grandmother, who must have been eighty-something, was probably the youngest of these **revolutionaries**.

"I'll come too!" he announced.

"Alfred, with respect, you are too young for such a dangerous mission."

The boy thought for a moment, before exclaiming, **"You are never too young for adventure!"**

There was another hurrah from the crew. This one was much more hesitant than the last.

"HURRAH!"

"That's my boy," said Grammy, patting her grandson on the head a little too hard for his liking.

PAT! PAT! PAT!

"Now, Enid, set a course for Big Ben!" announced the Old Queen.

"Aye, aye, Captain!" replied Enid, and the submarine **surged** through the water.

CHAPTER 34

A Carpet of Rats

Alfred was stationed at the periscope as the submarine snaked its way along the River Thames. Being underwater was the perfect cover for these **revolutionaries**. On **HMS** ***SCEPTRE***, they could move around London undetected. Soon the submarine had reached the Houses of Parliament. This gargantuan Gothic structure sat right on the River Thames. For hundreds of years it had been a place where politicians met to debate the important issues of the day.

Now there were **no politicians.**

No elections.

No democracy.

As a result, the Houses of Parliament were empty and

had fallen into total disrepair. The only part of the building that did still function was the clock tower, home of the bell known as "Big Ben". This chimed on the hour every hour, telling the people of London the time. Now that it was dark all day and all night, it was hard to tell if three chimes meant three in the afternoon or three in the morning. Still, it was one of the very last symbols of the old order that was still working. If Big Ben still struck on the hour, every hour, it gave the illusion that life was somehow normal. It was important to the Lord Protector, who kept the Houses of Parliament under armed guard at all times.

"Big Ben in sight, Grammy! I mean, Captain Grammy – I mean Captain," spluttered Alfred.

"Excellent work, sailor," replied the Old Queen. "Now, ladies, there are **revolutionaries** all over London, all over Britain, awaiting our signal. When Big Ben chimes thirteen times, that will send a message for miles around that the moment has finally arrived for **revolution!**"

"REVOLUTION!" chimed in the old dears together.

"I will lead a team of two ladies good and true to the base of the clock tower."

The Old Queen unrolled a diagram of the tower.

"From the intelligence we have gathered, the so-called royal guards are stationed here, here and here."

With her gloved finger, she indicated a number of places at the base and top of the tower.

"Our mission is to seize control of the bell tower itself at the stroke of midnight. A moment too soon and the guard will raise the alarm. A moment too late and we will have missed our chance. Instead of twelve strikes, we will change the clock's workings to strike thirteen. Once safely back here in **HMS *SCEPTRE***, we will be ready to launch the orb."

"Orb?" asked Alfred.

The Old Queen winked mischievously and paced over to a huge metal container. She whisked off a cover to reveal an antique torpedo with **"ORB"** emblazoned on it.

"Oh my goodness, Grammy!" exclaimed the boy. All of a sudden, he was terrified these old dears might blow themselves up, taking him with them.

"Beauty, isn't she?" said Grammy, patting the torpedo a little too hard for Alfred's liking. "This will blow a ruddy great hole in the side of the Tower of London, freeing all those innocent folk locked up there."

"I hope you know what you are doing, Grammy," remarked Alfred. "Mama is one of the prisoners."

"Of course we do, boy! Just look at my crack team! We are in our prime!"

"HURRAH!" chimed the old ladies together.

Their prime looked a while ago, but the prince said nothing. It wouldn't help.

"Enid!" called out the Old Queen.

"Yes, Captain?" she replied.

"You are coming with me and my boy. And Agatha!"

"Do I have to?" complained Agatha.

"Yes! Now, ladies…"

Alfred gave his grandmother a look.

"…and gentleman. Follow me!"

The ladies picked up their handbags.

What do the old dears need their handbags for? thought Alfred.

Next, Grammy grabbed a rusty old torch, then led the other three up the metal ladder and out of the submarine. The four of them stood wobbling on the bow of the vessel, as it gently rocked in the swell of the Thames. Alfred looked up at the clock tower, and took a deep breath. After all the bravado with the old ladies, he was beginning to feel sick with nerves.

"You tickety-boo, boy?" asked the Old Queen.

"Yes, Captain, ready for action," he lied.

She swung a rope with a hook at the end of it back and forth a few times. Then with all her might she threw it high into the air.

WHOOSH!

The end hooked on to a ledge of the Houses of Parliament.

CLUNK!

Grammy checked it was secure, then, looking smug with her handiwork, she hissed, "Still got it! Now, ladies, and, er, gentleman, follow me."

One by one, the three old dears used the rope to scale the river wall. Agatha put her walking stick between her teeth like a pirate might a cutlass as she climbed. Alfred went last, and before long the group found themselves inside the deserted chamber of the House of Commons.

The prince had seen pictures of this place in his history books. In the old days it was crowded with politicians. Now it had been ransacked. Windows had been smashed, and those distinctive green leather benches had been ripped, and the Speaker's chair upturned. When Alfred looked down at the floor, he realised something was very wrong.

"The carpet," he whispered. "It's moving."

The Old Queen answered, "Rats."

A sea of rats was rolling over the floor. Thousands of them.

"Let's get out of here," whispered the boy.

Grammy checked her little gold watch. "We have ten minutes until midnight. Move out!"

She gestured with her hand, and Enid and Agatha, who had been catching their breath, followed on.

They passed down hallway after hallway in the Houses of Parliament. Everywhere they stepped, rats scattered.

SCRATCH! SCRATCH!

SCRATCH!

No one said a word until the Old Queen walked straight into what she thought was a net.

"HELP!" she cried.

She had become tangled up in something that hung from one side of the wall to the other. It was only when the other three began untangling her that they realised what it was.

"A spider's web," said Alfred as he pulled the cobwebs off his grandmother.

"No one has been down here in years," muttered the Old Queen, brushing a giant spider over her shoulder as if it were a fleck of dandruff. "Onwards!"

They pressed on, illuminated only by the rusty old torch she was holding. As they neared a turn in the hallway, she placed her finger to her lips.

"What does that mean?" asked Enid.

"Be quiet, dear!" replied Agatha.

"SHUSH!" shushed Alfred.

"Oh!" exclaimed Enid. "Are we nearly there yet? I need a wee!"

"SHUSH!" shushed everyone.

Then the Old Queen flicked the switch on her torch and turned off the light.

FLICK!

As slowly and silently as she could, she peered round the corner. Alfred did too.

In the distance, shadows could be made out. On closer inspection, these were the silhouettes of two royal guards. They were guarding the door to the clock tower.

The Old Queen gently rolled her torch along the floor towards them.

CLANK! CLUNK! CLINK!

The two guards stepped towards the torch and peered down to inspect it. The Old Queen gave the signal, and the two old ladies knew exactly what to do. Enid and Agatha charged towards the guards.

"CHARGE!"

They whacked them over their heads with their handbags.

THWACK!

THWACK!

THWACK!

That's why they needed their handbags!

With the guards dazed and confused, Enid and Agatha attempted to wrestle their laser guns off them.

In the commotion, blasts of light shot from their guns, hitting the walls and ceiling.

ZAP!

ZAP!

ZAP!

BOOM!

BOOM!

BOOM!

Agatha must have been hit…

ZAP!

…as she collapsed to the floor in an instant.

THUD!

The Old Queen grabbed one of the guards from behind and trained his laser gun on the other. Alfred did the same and, in a glorious moment, the two guards zapped each other…

ZAP!

ZAP!

…and fell to the floor.

THUD!

THUD!

Immediately, attention turned to Agatha.

"Agatha? Agatha?" asked the Old Queen, as she began slapping the old dear around the face. "Wake up! Wake up! Oh dear, please, you're only ninety-two! This isn't your time to go!"

SLAP!

SLAP!

SLAP!

But, slap as she might, Agatha just wouldn't wake up. Tears welled in the Old Queen's eyes as she realised **the worst.**

CHAPTER 35

The Opposite of Vertigo

The Old Queen led a prayer.

"May our Lord take good care of this fallen hero. My lady-in-waiting Agatha was always there for me, to hold an unwanted bouquet of flowers, or pass me a bottle of hand cream, or take the blame for one of my particularly boisterous bottom burps."

As she tried to lay her friend to rest by closing her eyelids, Agatha woke up with a start.

"You poked me in the eye!" she protested.

"You're alive!" exclaimed the Old Queen.

"Yes! Of course I am alive! Now, for goodness' sake, help me up!"

Alfred, Enid and the Old Queen hoisted Agatha to her feet.

"Actually, I am feeling a little dizzy. Can I lie back down again?"

"There isn't time!" snapped the Old Queen. "Alfred?"

"Yes, Grammy?"

"Search the guards for keys."

With all his strength, Alfred rolled one of the guards over, and found a set of old iron keys on his belt.

"Here!" he said, holding them up.

JINGLE-
JANGLE!

"Excellent work!" she replied, and her grandson beamed with pride.

The Old Queen and Enid held on to the laser guns as Alfred led them to the door at the end of the hallway.

It bore the sign **CLOCK TOWER**.

Alfred put a key in the lock of the door, and success…

CLICK!

…the door opened.

Alfred tiptoed inside. Whatever the opposite of vertigo is, the boy instantly felt it as he looked up at the endless flights of stairs that led to the bell.

There were **342 steps!** He would never have been able to climb that many steps before, but now, somehow, it felt possible. He surged ahead, and with heavy hearts the old dears followed him. They had to go as quietly as they could, as it was likely there would be more armed guards stationed higher up the tower.

Nearing the top, they passed the giant clock face. It looked as big as the moon, and as bright as it too, illuminated as it was against the inky sky. For a moment, Alfred became lost, marvelling at it, before realising it was only a couple of minutes before twelve. There was no time to lose. They pressed on, nearing the room that housed the bell. As predicted, two more members of the royal guard stood by that door.

"Give this to Agatha," whispered Grammy. As she handed her laser gun to him, Alfred fumbled and the gun slipped out of his hand.

As if in slow motion, it began falling down the stairwell.

Silently at first and then inevitably…

CLUNK!

Spinning, it hit the balustrade.

CLUNK!

And again.

CLUNK!

Until it clattered all the way down to the floor below.

CLASH!

There was an eerie silence for a moment until the royal guards above leaped into action, blasting their laser guns down at the intruders.

ZAP! ZAP! ZAP!

CHAPTER 36

BONG!

Alfred and the three old dears clung to the wall of the clock tower to be out of the firing line of the guards.

ZAP! ZAP! ZAP!

WOOH! WOOH! WOOH!

A deafening siren sounded. The game was up.

"Let's run back to the submarine!" shouted Enid over the racket.

"We can't!" said Alfred.

"NEVER SURRENDER!" announced the Old Queen.

With that, she took the last remaining laser gun from Enid and charged up the stairs with the blaster in her gloved hand.

ZAP! ZAP! ZAP!

From below, Alfred watched with a combination of horror and awe as first one royal guard, then another, plunged down the stairwell.

CLUNK!
CLUNK!
THUD!
THUD!

"ONWARD!" shouted the Old Queen, waving the blaster above her head as if it were a sword. "I haven't had this much fun since that man streaked at Royal Ascot!"

Alfred and the two ladies-in-waiting followed, gathering themselves behind the Old Queen as she blasted the door to the belfry open.

ZAP!
KABOOM!

The smoke cleared to reveal Big Ben in all its glory. This gigantic bronze-and-tin bell, weighing more than a double-decker bus, was moments from being struck by the giant hammer that made it sound.

Four smaller bells chimed the little tune that always came before the bongs.

DAH DEE DUM DUM DAH DEE DUM DUM DAH DEE DUM DUM DAH DEE DUM DUM…

Then the BONGs began.

BONG!

"To the hammer!" commanded the Old Queen.

BONG!

Next to the bell was the huge hammer.

BONG!

It sat on an arm that reached round the bell.

BONG!

And struck the bell mechanically.

BONG!

"How the devil are we going to make it strike thirteen times?" asked Enid.

BONG!

"I think I know a way!" replied Alfred.

BONG!

The boy leaped up and clambered on to the arm.

BONG!

Immediately he felt how strong the reverberations were, and-d-d b-b-began t-t-to w-w-wonder w-w-whether h-h-he c-c-could-d-d k-k-keep h-h-holding-g-g on-n-n!

BONG!

His entire body was SSSHHHHAAAAK KKIIINNNGGG!

BONG!

Still Alfred shuffled down the arm.

BONG!

"H-h-how m-m-many b-b-bongs w-w-was th-th-that?" he called out.

BONG!

"Twelve!" replied Grammy. "NOW!"

The boy leaped down on to the hammer, forcing all his weight on to it.

BONG!

YES! He had done it! Big Ben had struck thirteen times! The signal had been given. The time for REVOLUTION was NOW!

Alfred beamed from ear to ear, even as his head s-h-h-o-o-o-o-k-k as the sound travelled through him. He leaped off the arm and back on to the platform.

"Excellent work, young prince!" exclaimed Grammy, embracing the boy.

"Thank you," replied Alfred.

"That will have been heard across London. Word will spread throughout this country. The revolution has begun!"

"HURRAH!" cried out Enid and Agatha.

But their celebration was short-lived.

The four turned round to see that they were surrounded by a platoon of royal guards pointing their blasters at them.

This was the end.

CHAPTER 37

Hotty Botty

One of the guards gestured for the Old Queen to put her weapon down.

The other three looked at her.

Grammy was no fool and dropped the blaster on to the floor.

CLATTER!

Another guard approached slowly and picked up the blaster as the others all kept their weapons trained on the gang.

Then one guard gestured for them to make their way

out of the belfry and down the stairs.

Soon the gang of four had reached the narrow room that ran alongside one of the giant clock faces. The hands of the clock turned on a giant black rod, which they passed under as they walked.

Agatha still had her walking stick, and Alfred had a bright idea.

DING!

"Let me borrow this," he hissed, and without a word she handed it to him.

As he passed under the rod, he scrambled up his grandmother's back. Then, hooking the end of the walking stick on to the rod, Alfred swung towards the guards.

WHOOSH!

His foot clipped the helmet of the first one.

CLONK!

One by one, they knocked each other over.

CLONK! CLONK! CLONK!

In no time, they were lying in a heap on the floor.

"RUN!" ordered the Old Queen.

As fast as they could, which wasn't really that fast, they made their way out of the clock room, and slammed the door shut behind them.

SCHTUM!

BANG! BANG! BANG!

The guards all hammered on the door, but Agatha grabbed her walking stick and jammed it into the lock, keeping it closed.

SHONT!

Looking down over the balustrade, the Old Queen spied more guards now waiting at the bottom of the stairs for them.

ZAP! ZAP! ZAP!

BOOM!

The door behind them was being blasted open.

"We're trapped!" exclaimed Grammy.

"I have an idea," said Alfred. "Follow me!"

He climbed on to the banister, and began sliding down as fast as he could go.

WHOOSH!

One by one, the three old dears followed.

WHOOSH!

WHOOSH!

WHOOSH!

"WAHEE!"

exclaimed Enid.

"THIS IS FABULOUS!"

added Agatha.

"MY BOTTY IS HOTTY!"

hollered Grammy. "AND I LIKE IT!"

The royal guards fired their weapons up at them.

ZAP!

ZAP!

ZAP!

But they were going so fast they were impossible to hit.

Instead plaster exploded from the walls.

BOOM! BOOM! BOOM!

The guards at the bottom of the stairs didn't stand a chance.

WHACK!

Alfred flew SLAP BANG into them, knocking them over.

CLONK! CLONK! CLONK!

THUD! THUD! THUD!

The three old ladies stepped over them as they raced out of the clock tower and back into the Houses of Parliament. Retracing their steps, they twisted and turned along the maze of hallways, into the chamber, until they finally reached the smashed window through which they had entered.

"GO! GO! GO!" ordered the Old Queen, making sure she was the last to leave.

The four slid down the rope and landed back on the bow of HMS *SCEPTRE*.

“We did it, Grammy!” said the boy.

“You did it, Alfred!” she replied. “Now to the Tower!”

But, just as they were hurrying back inside the submarine, something parted the black clouds in the sky and loomed over them. It was the airship!

“Oh no!” said Alfred.

A flurry of laser shots rained down from above.

ZAP!

ZAP!

ZAP!

The Old Queen was hit in the back.

"AHH!" she cried as she fell face forward into the black water.

SPLASH!

"***NOOOOOO!***" screamed Alfred.

CHAPTER 38

Life & Death

Grammy was floating face down in the water. Alfred rushed to the side of the submarine, as laser blast after laser blast scorched the hull of HMS *SCEPTRE* from the airship above.

ZAP! ZAP! ZAP! ZAP! ZAP!

BOOM! BOOM! BOOM! BOOM! BOOM!

"GRAMMY!" he cried as he tried to slide down into the water to reach her.

Enid yanked him back.

"I know you love her, but you can't help her now," she implored. "Get inside before you are blasted to pieces too."

"NO!" cried the boy.

ZAP! ZAP! ZAP! ZAP! ZAP!

BOOM! BOOM! BOOM! BOOM! BOOM!

"YOU ARE COMING WITH ME!" ordered Enid, and she dragged Alfred inside the submarine as laser blasts rained down all around them.

"GRAMMY!"

ZAP! ZAP! ZAP! ZAP! ZAP!

BOOM! BOOM! BOOM! BOOM! BOOM!

Once inside, HMS *SCEPTRE* lurched off at speed as more laser blasts hit the hull.

ZAP! ZAP! ZAP!

BOOM! BOOM! BOOM!

Tears rolled down Alfred's face.

"I can't believe Grammy's gone," he sobbed.

"The Old Queen died how she would have wanted to," spluttered a tearful Agatha. "A hero."

"Much better to die a hero than live as a coward," remarked Enid, choking back her tears.

"Shot in the back!" said Alfred.

"But with her head held high!" continued a distraught Enid. "The best way we can honour her now is to complete her mission. We must save this country. I speak for all us ladies when I say we will serve you now, Prince Alfred. We await your orders, sir."

They all looked to the boy. Alfred took a deep breath. He was not ready for this. Not ready at all. He was only twelve, and still in his pyjamas. But now was the moment for him to embrace his destiny.

"To the Tower!"

All the old ladies rushed to their posts on the submarine. Alfred stood up, dried his eyes on his sleeve and resumed his position by the periscope. It took all his strength just to stand there, and not collapse to the floor with grief. He had never felt more broken.

"Is the target in sight, sir?" asked Agatha.

"Yes. The Tower of London is in sight," replied the boy.

"Shall we load the torpedo?" said Enid.

Alfred looked down at the orb ready to be wheeled into position. He hesitated. His mother was still locked in the Tower.

"Are you positive that thing isn't going to blow the whole place to smithereens?"

"Just a hole, sir," replied Enid. "A big one, but a hole. It is meant to take down a destroyer. Not a city."

"And all the prisoners would have heard the thirteen chimes," added Agatha. "They know it is coming. What would you like us to do, sir?"

For the first time in his life, Alfred realised that life and death was in his hands. The responsibility of being a prince, and leader of men – or, rather, old ladies – was upon him.

"Load the torpedo!" he ordered.

The ladies-in-waiting struggled with the weight of it, and Alfred went to help them. Just like the submarine itself, the torpedo dated back to World War One. It was battered and cracked, and Alfred wondered whether it would go off. It was two hundred years old, after all.

Lifting it from the cradle, Agatha cried out, "Oh! My back's gone!"

The torpedo slipped out of her hands. Just as it was about to smash on to the floor, and goodness knows what…

KAAAABOOOOOMMM?

...Alfred took the extra weight just in time.

"Phew," exclaimed Enid.

"Phew indeed," agreed the boy.

With great care, the torpedo was loaded into the tube.

"**ORB** is ready to launch!" announced Agatha.

Alfred gulped before making the announcement. "FIRE!"

Then...

NOTHING HAPPENED.

NOTHING AT ALL.

NOT A SAUSAGE.

NOTHING.

"Sorry!" said Agatha. "I think I left the safety catch on."

She flicked a switch.

CLICK!

"Oh dear. Right! Ready!"

"FIRE!" commanded Alfred again.

This time he could feel something was happening. The entire submarine rattled. Then…

BANG!

The torpedo shot from the cylinder.

Through the periscope, Alfred could make it out, surging down the river…

WHOOSH!

before…

KABOOM!

It hit the Tower of London and exploded.

In an instant, the ancient building was in flames.

Smoke billowed across the river. Through it, Alfred could make out figures diving into the water below.

"TO THE SURFACE!" he ordered.

As soon as the submarine had ascended, Alfred raced up the ladder and leaped on to the hull. He was desperate to spot his mother in amongst all the prisoners leaping from the burning building into the River Thames.

SPLISH!

SPLASH!

SPLOSH!

Most were swimming to the far side of the river. Alfred spotted a figure behind the others. He remembered his mother could not swim very well. He plunged into the water…

SPLOSH!

…and swam over to her.

"Mama!" he called.

"*Lionheart!* I knew you'd save me!" she replied.

Bobbing in the water, she held him close.

"I love you," he said.

"I love you too."

The Queen held her son even tighter, and their heads went under the water.

BLUB! BLUB! BLUB!

"You nearly drowned me!" exclaimed Alfred.

"I am sorry. *I just love you too much.*"

"Come on!" said Alfred. He took her hand and together they swam towards the submarine.

When they had reached the relative safety of the vessel, they heaved themselves up on to it.

"Where is Grammy?" asked his mother, looking around.

Alfred shook his head. He couldn't bear to say it.

"Gone?" she asked.

The boy nodded his head.

"No!" Tears welled in the Queen's eyes. "No. Not dear old Grammy. How did she die?"

"Shot in the back."

"I am sorry. I know how much you loved her."

"Oh, I did. I really did."

"And I know how much she loved you. There will always be a part of Grammy inside you – never forget that."

"I won't, Mama."

Just then a small voice in the water cried out, "D-d-don't forget about m-m-me!"

Alfred squinted to make out who it was.

"M-M-MITE!" he cried.

Together he and the Queen hauled her out of the water.

"Thanks!" said the little girl. "I thought I was a goner."

Laser blasts began exploding all around them.

ZAP! ZAP! ZAP! ZAP! ZAP!

BOOM! BOOM! BOOM! BOOM! BOOM!

The three held on tight to the hull as HMS *SCEPTRE* powered away from the blazing Tower of London.

Alfred saluted.

"Goodbye, Grammy," he said as her body drifted down the river.

CHAPTER 39

Limb from Limb

All along the riverbank, people came out of their hiding places.

They had heard the thirteen bongs of Big Ben.

They were ready for **REVOLUTION!**

On seeing the submarine surging along the Thames, with a Union Jack flying from its hull, cheers went up across London.

"HOORAY!"

The poor. The hungry. The homeless. Now was their time to fight back against the evil regime that had kept them living in fear for so long. They waved their own Union Jack flags high in the air.

With a loudspeaker, the Queen spoke from the hull of the submarine: "It is time for the Lord Protector's evil dictatorship to end! We will tear down the flag of the griffin, and replace it with the flag of our great nation!"

"HOORAY!"

A portly man of Indian descent called out from the riverbank. He was waving a severely out-of-date bag of marshmallows, and shouting, "Anyone looking for a special offer on some delicious mallowmarshes?"

It was FUTURE RAJ! He was exactly the same as normal Raj, but his confectionery was even more out of date.

"Smile and wave, dear," prompted the Queen. "Smile and wave. That's what we royals do."

Alfred, not used to being out in public, did as his mother said, even though it felt a bit silly.

ZAP! ZAP! ZAP!

It felt even sillier when more laser blasts from the airship above hit the submarine.

BOOM! BOOM! BOOM!

The Lord Protector's flying machine was chasing them.

"QUICKLY! INSIDE! NOW!" shouted the boy, and he held his mother's and Mite's hands and led them down inside HMS *SCEPTRE* to safety.

The ladies-in-waiting found blankets for the two new arrivals and wrapped them up tight.

"The last time I saw you, Nanny was taking you to the palace kitchen to get some chocolate," began Alfred. "How did you end up locked in the Tower of London?"

The little girl was shivering with cold. "I d-d-didn't g-g-get n-n-no ch-ch-chocolate!"

"No?"

"I w-w-waited and-d-d w-w-waited. Th-th-then, n-n-next th-th-thing I kn-kn-know, the-the-the r-r-room is-s-s f-f-full of-f-f g-g-guards!"

The Queen began listening to the conversation.

"That's strange," said Alfred.

"Is-s-s it-t-t?" asked Mite.

Did the little girl know something he didn't?

"Yes," joined in the Queen. "It is strange. Nanny has been in the royal household for all her working life. She looked after my little *Lionheart* here."

With that, she looked lovingly at her son and stroked his hair.

Alfred glowed with embarrassment that his mother was doing this in front of the girl.

"I d-d-don't tr-tr-trust her one b-b-bit," said Mite.

The boy went deep into his mind.

There were some things about Nanny that were hard to explain.

Why did he feel so much better now he wasn't eating her **eggy-wegg** every morning?

Why did Nanny insist on locking him in his bedroom?

Why did she not believe him about the statue of the griffin being used in the ritual, even when he found his father's blood on it?

As quickly as Alfred had had these thoughts, he dismissed them. Nanny had cared for him since he was a baby, the King before him too – there was no way she could be involved in the Lord Protector's evil plans. The last Alfred had heard, the wicked man was interrogating her!

"Where to, Captain?" asked Enid, waking the boy up from his daydream.

"Buckingham Palace!" replied the prince. "Full speed ahead. We must get there before all of London does."

"Goodness, yes," agreed the Queen. "I fear the

angry mob will tear my husband limb from limb. They will blame the King for this tyrannical rule, and not the real villain, the Lord Protector."

"We must save the King," called out the prince.

"Full speed ahead to the palace!" shouted Agatha.

Alfred took his place at the periscope. Looking through it, he spied platoons of royal guards taking positions on Westminster Bridge. If the gang tried to disembark from the submarine at that point, there would be a massacre.

"Blast!" said the prince. "We are not going to be able to get close to the palace."

"It's impossible," agreed the Queen.

There were murmurs of agreement from the old dears.

Mite spoke up. "It's not impossible. I know a way."

"You don't mean…?" began Alfred.

"The Tube tunnel I swam up!" exclaimed the girl.

"But would a submarine fit?"

"It should do," she replied. "This thing is about the same size as one of those old Tube trains. I just need to show you the place where the tunnel meets the Thames."

Enid unrolled a map of London, and Mite began trying to make sense of it all. Finally, she pointed to a spot and shouted, "THERE! RIGHT OPPOSITE THE LONDON EYE!"

The ladies all gathered around to study the map.

"There, deep under the water level, is a giant hole. It must have been created by an explosion. That's the way into the Tube tunnel!"

All the old dears shook their heads.

"What?" demanded Mite.

"YOU CAN'T PILOT A SUBMARINE UP THE Piccadilly Line!" exclaimed Enid.

"If it's wide enough, then why not?" asked Alfred. "Otherwise, we'll be nothing but target practice for the royal guards."

"That's a big if," muttered Agatha.

"Look," began Alfred, "we don't have time to argue about this. For all we know, the griffin could be about to destroy all of London!"

There were mutters of agreement from all the ladies-in-waiting.

"The prince is right," said Enid.

"Ladies!" began Agatha. "Let's do this!"

"To your stations!" commanded Alfred.

"That's my boy!" the Queen proclaimed proudly.

In moments, **HMS *SCEPTRE*** was surging through the water towards the entrance to the Tube tunnel.

Using the ancient radar…

BEEP! BEEP! BEEP!

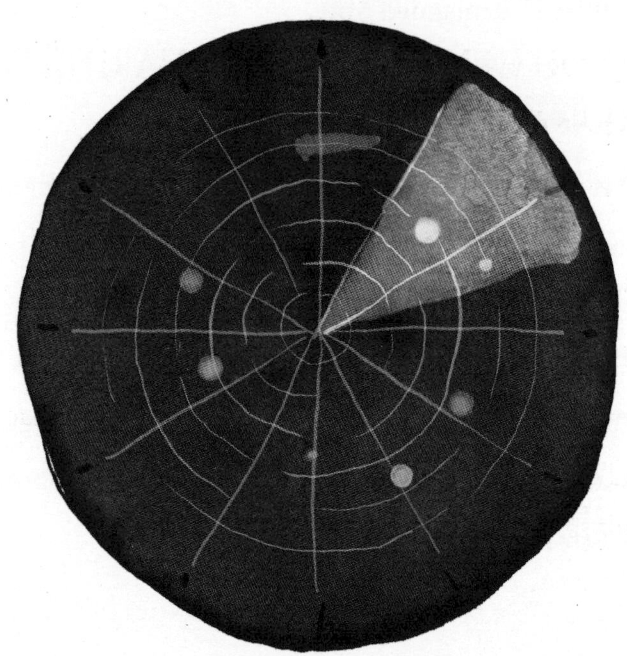

…the exact location of the hole was found.

It was just, just, just wider than HMS *SCEPTRE* herself.

Expert navigation was needed to prevent the submarine from becoming jammed. If HMS *SCEPTRE* did become stuck, then they would all die a slow and painful death.

"Hold tight, ladies!" called out the prince. "We're going in!"

DUMF!

The submarine shuddered as it scraped the side of the entrance to the tunnel.

All eyes turned to the prince, who was trying his best to keep his cool.

CRUNCH!

Another knock.

"HOLD HER STEADY!" he ordered.

Enid held the steering wheel tightly, sweat pouring from her brow. Agatha mopped it up with a lace handkerchief.

DUNK!

Another hit.

"Hold her steady."

The submarine began passing up the Tube tunnel itself.

"HURRAH!" shouted the ladies.

The plan was working.

HMS *SCEPTRE* edged closer and closer to the palace.

Then... KERRUNCH!

The submarine lurched to a halt.

Horror upon horror, they were stuck!

"BACKWARDS!" ordered the prince.

There was a deafening grinding noise.

GGGGGRRRRR!

But the submarine didn't budge.

CRUNCH!

"FORWARD!"

Again, there was nothing but an earsplitting noise.

GGGGGRRRRR!

GRONCH!

"BACKWARDS!"

GGGGGRRRRR!

KERRUMPH!

It didn't move an inch.

Then, in an instant, the submarine was plunged into

DARKNESS.

The lights on board had failed.

They were doomed.

CHAPTER 40

Doomed

"Everyone stay calm!" commanded the prince. It was little use. Panic was spreading through the submarine like wildfire.

"CALM!" exclaimed Enid. "We're stuck!" She checked the dial on the air supply. "And we only have an hour until the air supply runs out!"

"Please just stay calm," implored Alfred.

"You already said that!"

"It was all my stupid idea," said Mite. "I should take the blame. Not him."

Agatha found a box of the Old Queen's matches and struck one.

STRIKE!

That at least gave a flicker of light inside the submarine.

Then... **DISASTER!**

All that could be heard for a few moments was the creaking of the HMS *SCEPTRE*'s hull.

TWANG! TWONG! TWUNG!

It sounded like the ancient submarine was going to snap in two!

"ARGH!"

"NOOO!"

"HELP!"

Screams rang through the gloom.

"Oh, Mama, I've failed," sniffed Alfred.

The Queen reached out in the darkness for her son.

"Don't say that," she replied, gripping his hand tight. "This isn't over yet. There must be a way out of the submarine."

"I am so, so sorry," said Mite.

"Over here!" ordered Enid.

Agatha brought the flickering flame to the ladder, and Enid scaled it, holding a hammer. After a good deal of banging and bashing…

CLUNK!

CLINK!

CLANK!

…she came back down the ladder and turned to the Queen.

"I am sorry, Your Majesty, but you're wrong," said Enid sorrowfully. "It's impossible to open the hatch from the inside, and there is no other way out of the submarine."

"So, we are doomed?" asked Agatha.

"Yes, my dear. Doomed," replied Enid.

"It's all my fault," said Mite.

There was silence for a moment, before the prince broke it.

"The torpedo launcher!" he exclaimed.

"I beg your pardon!" replied Enid.

"If you can launch a torpedo, then maybe you can launch me!"

"Preposterous!"

"Nonsense!"

"The boy has lost his marbles!" muttered the old dears.

"It's not preposterous!" snapped Alfred. "I'm about the same size as a torpedo!"

Alfred was small for his age.

"It's too dangerous!" announced his mother. "It is certain death."

"But staying here is certain death…" reasoned Alfred.

"Being shot out of a cannon is an even more certain death," remarked Enid.

"How can it be even MORE certain?" asked the boy.

This rather stumped Enid, who shut up.

Agatha took over. "Forgive me, but I think what my fellow lady-in-waiting meant was that being shot out of a torpedo tube is a faster way to die. But, and this is a big but, if you survived it, there is a chance you could open the hatch from the outside."

"*As your future king,*" announced Prince Alfred grandly, "*I am willing to try!*"

"I am too!" said Mite.

"You ruined my big moment!" he complained. "I was being all royal and heroic."

"I don't care. Listen! I'm a really good swimmer. Let me come too! I can help!"

"All right, all right!" replied Alfred.

"Good boy!" said the Queen.

"Splendid! Then I suggest that your girlfriend—" began Agatha.

"She's not my girlfriend!" snapped the boy.

"He's not my boyfriend!" snapped the girl. "I would rather eat my own foot than go out with him!"

"And I would rather eat my own –" Alfred was struggling to think of something worse-tasting than foot – "BOTTOM!"

Enid looked as if she might faint at this rude word. Agatha reached for a bottle of smelling salts and wafted them under her friend's nose.

"I suggest your friend," continued Agatha, "who happens to be a girl, but is definitely not your girlfriend, goes first."

"YES!" exclaimed Mite, victorious.

"In case she is crushed to death, being fired out of the torpedo tube."

"Oh," said the girl. "On second thoughts, Prince, you can go first!"

"ME?" said the boy.

"Yes. You are royal, after all!" With that, she did a little flourish with her hand, mocking the whole cavalcade of royalty in one tiny gesture.

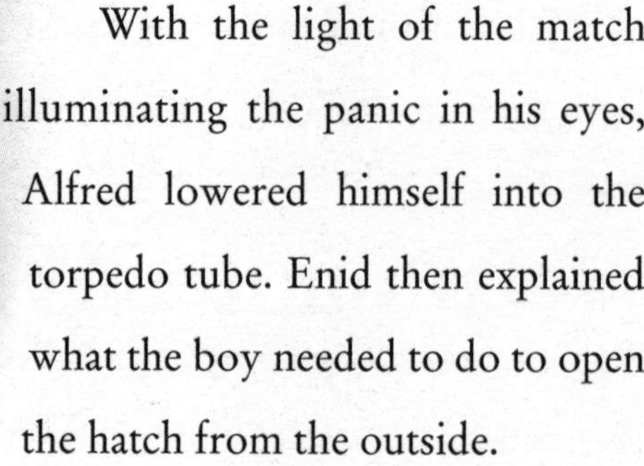

With the light of the match illuminating the panic in his eyes, Alfred lowered himself into the torpedo tube. Enid then explained what the boy needed to do to open the hatch from the outside.

"Turn the left lever anti-clockwise."

The boy nodded his head – he had sort of understood.

"Torpedo – I mean, boy – ready to fire!" called out Enid.

"*I love you forever, Lionheart,*" whispered the Queen.

"*I love you forever, Mama.*

FIRE AT WILL!"

BOOM!

WHOOSH!

Alfred was blasted out of the submarine.

CHAPTER 41

Human Torpedo

WwwwwwOOOOOooooo SSSSSSSSSSHHHHHHHHHH!

Alfred was being propelled through the water so fast he thought he was going to end up in outer space. The water in the **Underground** tunnel was black and he had no clue whether he was upside down or inside out.

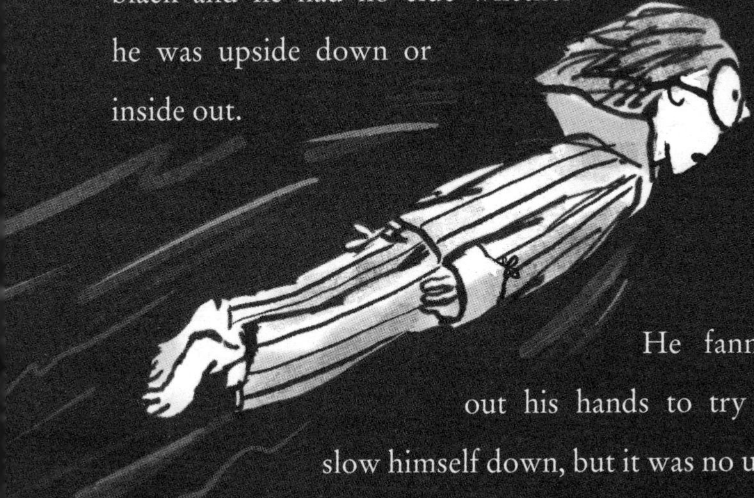

He fanned out his hands to try to slow himself down, but it was no use.

THUD!

His body was hurled against an underwater wall.

Alfred grimaced at the pain, but no bones were broken. He pushed himself up and away from the wall, and gulped a mouthful of much-needed air at the surface.

GASP!

He was alive.

Just.

Right ahead of him he saw a half-submerged sign that read **GREEN PARK.**

It was an ancient platform notice. If they had reached what once was **Green Park Underground** station, they were now very near Buckingham Palace.

An old vending machine bobbed in the water.

PLOP! PLOP! PLOP!

Such a shame I don't have a 50p piece to buy a chocolate bar, thought Alfred, who was starving.

There was a faint glimmer of light dancing on the surface of the water. Not far off, he could just make out the outline of the HMS *SCEPTRE*. He could see that the vessel was at an angle, which was why it had become stuck in the tunnel.

At once, he began swimming towards the submarine.

Then WHOOSH!

Mite shot out of the torpedo tube and smashed SLAP BANG into him.

BASH!

"ARGH!" he cried.

"That was COOL!" exclaimed Mite.

"I am still alive – thank you for asking," said Alfred sarcastically.

"Come on!" said the girl, and she powered through the water towards the submarine, leaving him flailing behind.

Just as he was catching up, Alfred felt something bashing and scratching at his head.

BOSH! BOSH! BOSH!

He turned round to see a cloud of bats flying towards him!

SQUEAK! SQUEAK! SQUEAK!

"ARGH! BATS!" he screamed.

"Yes. I should have mentioned them," said Mite. "The place is crawling with them."

SQUEAK! SQUEAK! SQUEAK!

Alfred dived so he could shake them off. After a few strokes, he'd reached Mite back at the submarine.

"Look! This is the hatch here," she said.

"Now did Enid say the right lever or the left? And was it clockwise? Or anticlockwise?" asked Alfred.

"I wasn't listening."

"I thought you were."

"That was the boring bit."

"Oh, for goodness' sake! You take that one, and I'll take this one."

After they had both yanked their levers to and fro for what seemed like an age, eventually the hatch opened.

CLUNK!

SUCCESS!

There were cheers from the ladies below deck.

"HURRAH!"

One by one, they began climbing on to the surface.

The Queen.

Enid.

Agatha.

Virginia.

Beatrix.

Daphne.

Judith.

"Thank you, son! You saved us all," said the Queen.

"You took your time!" remarked Enid.

"Now, can you all swim?" asked Alfred.

"Doggy paddle, yes," replied Agatha. "I have my twenty-five-metre badge."

"Then let's go," commanded the prince.

Together, they swam towards the light at the end of the tunnel.

The light grew dark, as if a thundercloud had passed over it.

"I should warn you," began Mite. "We need to look out for—"

But before Mite could say "bats" the swarm of creatures dive-bombed them.

SQUEAK! SQUEAK! SQUEAK!

As much as the old ladies attempted to bat the bats away with their hands, still the creatures attacked without mercy.

"ARGH!"

"GET OFF!"

"FLYING RAT!"

"SUBMERGE!" ordered the prince.

One by one, their heads bobbed under the water, and they swam as far as they could below the surface.

As soon as any of them bobbed up for air, the bats would strike again.

SQUEAK! SQUEAK! SQUEAK!

Eventually they reached the underneath of Buckingham Palace.

"Where are the steps that lead up to the palace vault, Mite?" asked Alfred.

"I'm trying to find them."

"Well, please try to find them a little bit faster!" called Agatha. "I'm not sure how much longer I can tread water! I never got my badge for that!"

Mite's hands scoured the top of the Underground tunnel, until she finally found the bottom step.

"HERE!" she exclaimed.

One by one, they hauled themselves on to the steps. Then they scrambled up them until they reached the top.

Above them was the large stone in the floor of the vault. Together the prince and Mite pushed it up and aside.

CLUNK!

Alfred climbed up first, and then helped the others into the palace vault.

Little did they know who was waiting for them, looming in the shadows…

CHAPTER 42

A Trap

"Oh, *my little prince!*" exclaimed Nanny, who had been waiting for them in the vault. The old lady hobbled over to the boy and held him tight.

"Hello, Nanny," said Alfred.

"I was so, so worried about you, being taken to the Tower and all," she said.

Mite looked on, mightily unimpressed by this show of affection. "Remember me?" she asked sarcastically.

"Oh yes, dear little Mite! One moment you were standing there in the kitchen while I went to fetch the chocolate. And the next moment you were gone! Where oh where did you get to?"

Mite shook her head, unmoved by this performance.

"An army of guards burst in and dragged me kicking and screaming to the Tower!"

"NO!"

"Yes!"

"Oh! I was so, so worried about you disappearing like that. Please tell me you are all right!" pleaded Nanny, bending down to stroke the little girl's cheek.

"I'm fine! No thanks to you," snapped the girl, batting the old lady's hand away.

Nanny bristled at this, but the Queen, standing behind the girl, provided a perfect distraction. The old lady did a little curtsey.

"Your Majesty."

"Nanny," replied the Queen, nodding her head politely. "How is the King?"

"Tut-tut-tut! Ooh, not good, Your Majesty. Not too good at all. He sent me down here to find you," said Nanny. "The King needs you all to come up to the ballroom at once."

Alfred was suspicious. "But how did you know we'd break into the palace this way?"

Nanny thought for a moment. "Mite showed us both this secret way in, remember? I am not as daft as I look! Ha! Ha! Now, come on," she continued. "There is no time to lose! *My little prince*, you be sure to stay close to me."

The old lady hobbled off through the maze of boxes and crates in the vault, holding the boy's hand tightly in hers.

A little too tightly. Nanny's grip was so strong it was actually painful.

"Nanny, your nails are digging into my hand," said Alfred, wincing.

"I just don't want you to let go is all," she replied.

The Queen, Mite and the six ladies-in-waiting followed on not far behind.

Then Nanny did the strangest thing. As she and Alfred passed behind a mighty metal box, she yanked him down to the floor.

"OW!"

Alfred was stunned. Then it dawned on him what was happening.

"IT'S A TRAP!" he shouted to the others.

At that moment from behind boxes and crates dotted all over the vast vault, a dozen or so royal guards revealed themselves. The soldiers had been hiding there all along. Their lasers were drawn, and immediately they began firing at the **revolutionaries** without mercy.

ZAP! ZAP! ZAP!

BOOM! BOOM! BOOM!

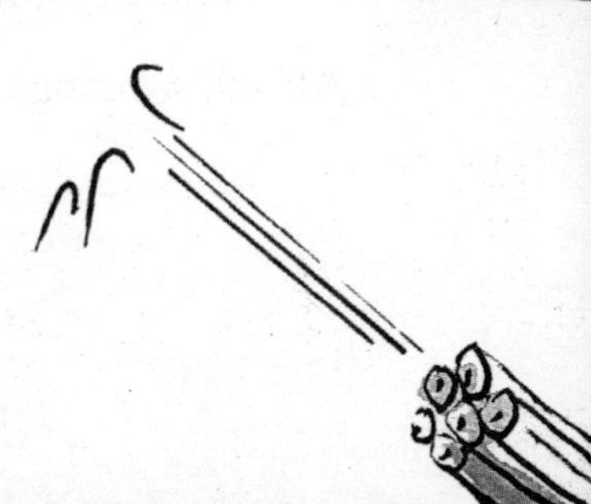

CHAPTER 43

Deadly Weapons

Mite and the Queen managed to duck down just in time. They hid behind an old leather trunk, as laser blasts skimmed over their heads.

ZAP! ZAP! ZAP!

BOOM! BOOM! BOOM!

"I knew that evil old witch was in on it!" hissed Mite over the noise.

"But why?" asked the Queen.

The ladies-in-waiting sprang into action. Immediately they began arming themselves with the treasures in the vault. Down here there were all kinds of deadly weapons. They found **swords** and **axes** and sabres and **spears** and flails.*

* THE FLAILS WERE THE DEADLIEST OF ALL: A SPIKED METAL BALL ATTACHED TO A HANDLE BY A CHAIN. THIS COULD DO AN AWFUL LOT OF DAMAGE.

Enid found a helmet and breastplate from a medieval suit of armour, which she hastily threw on to lead an attack on the royal guards.

"CHARGE!" she ordered, flailing a flail above her head.

The zaps of the laser guns bounced off the metal of her armour.

ZAP! ZAP! ZAP!

TING! TING! TING!

She clonked one of the guards over the head with the metal ball as hard as she could.

CLUNK!

"AAH!"

Meanwhile, Agatha was taking the army of guards on with not one, but two samurai swords!

CLINK! CLANK! CLUNK!

"COME ON!" she shouted over the din.

The old dears were fighting back!

Meanwhile, Alfred was trying with all his strength to escape Nanny's grip.

As he fought to get away, he saw the old lady's face contort into what she really was.

Pure evil.

"LET ME GO!" shouted the boy.

"OH NO!" she cried. "The Lord Protector has plans for you, *my little prince!*"

In desperation, he bit her hand.

"OWWW!" And she released her grip.

On his hands and knees, Alfred began to flee across the floor.

ZAP! ZAP! ZAP!

BOOM! BOOM! BOOM!

The old lady grabbed him by the ankles and dragged him back.

"ARGH!"

Alfred attempted to kick his way out of her clutches.

"GET OFF ME!"

But she pinned him to the stone floor with her

hands and knees. "I poisoned you all these years with my **eggy-wegg**!"

"You evil old witch!" snarled the prince. "I knew it tasted off!"

"It was off. Very off. So you would be nothing more than a sickly child. Unable to cause any trouble. Not even able to get out of bed. No threat to the Lord Protector's magnificent scheme!"

IT WAS TRUE! Alfred went red with rage!

"You monster! But why have you done all this? You haven't told me why! WHY?"

Nanny smiled, revealing her false teeth. "None of you have ever worked it out, have you?"

"Worked out what?" demanded the prince.

"That I have a son."

"A son?"

"Oh yes!"

"Who?"

"You still can't guess!"

CHAPTER 44

The Secret

"The **Lord Protector!**" exclaimed Alfred.

"The very same!" declared Nanny.

This was a complete surprise to Alfred, as it would be to everybody else in Buckingham Palace. Over forty years, the evil pair had never betrayed for a moment that they were mother and son.

ZAP! ZAP! ZAP!

BOOM! BOOM! BOOM!

"It's true. I brought him into the palace as a young man. He worked as a librarian at first. Devoured every book in the palace library. Found ancient magic books and all sorts. Dark arts. Discovered that the blood of the King might just raise a beast from the dead. My boy is clever. Cleverer than any of you.

He is a genius! My son yearned for power, and I encouraged him every step of the way. Soon he will be supreme ruler of this country, if not the world, with me, his mother, at his side!"

"Never!" shouted Alfred. **"This country belongs to all of us, not just you!"**

"He will. Trust me. He will. All we need is some of your royal blood!"

ZAP! ZAP! ZAP!

BOOM! BOOM! BOOM!

"NO!" snapped Alfred. "I have seen what your evil son has done to my father! You are not having a drop!"

"Oh yes I am," she purred. "And I will take it! Your blood is ours!"

With that, Nanny took out a jewel-handled dagger! She raised it high above her head, ready to bring it down upon the boy.

Alfred put his hands up to stop her, and at once they were engaged in a deadly arm wrestle.

ZAP! ZAP! ZAP!

BOOM! BOOM! BOOM!

Nanny edged the knife nearer and nearer to the boy's heart.

"NO!" cried Alfred, and he used all his strength to repel her.

Then the strangest thing happened.

In an instant, the light in Nanny's eyes went out.

She dropped the dagger…

CLANK!

…and slumped down on to the stone floor beside him.

THUD!

Dead.

Now Alfred could see that Nanny had a sabre sticking out of her back.

Looking up, he saw that standing over her body was the Queen.

"Don't you dare hurt my son!" she said.

"Thank you, Mama," said Alfred.

"Anything for you, *Lionheart*."

Mite scuttled over to join them. "I never did like that woman," she remarked.

ZAP! ZAP! ZAP!

BOOM! BOOM! BOOM!

There was the sound of a scream.

"ARGH!"

It was Enid! She'd been hit.

"ENID!" cried Alfred as he crawled over to her.

"You go, boy," replied the old dear. "Defeat this monster. We ladies-in-waiting will do our best to hold the guards down here in the vault!"

"But what about you?" asked Alfred.

"Don't you worry about me. What was it the Old Queen said? **'You are never too old for adventure!'** I wouldn't have missed this for the world."

Alfred nodded to Mite and the Queen, and together the three scuttled off on their hands and knees out of the line of fire.

ZAP! ZAP! ZAP!

BOOM! BOOM! BOOM!

Just then the OCTOBUT appeared through the door of the vault, holding a tennis racquet. It still had only two of its eight arms left.

"Anyone for tennis?" it asked.

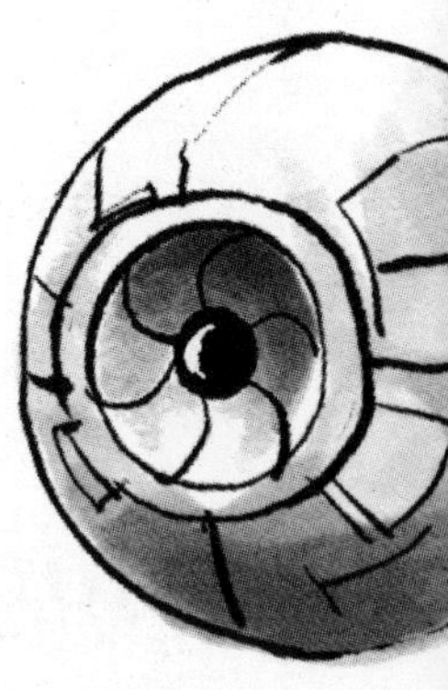

One of the royal guards turned round sharply and blasted another one of its arms clean off.

ZAP!

CLANK!

The arm holding the tennis racquet was twitching on the floor.

The robot butler only had one lonely arm left. It was now really a Unibut.

"Thank you, OCTOBUT!" called out Alfred.

Brilliantly, the accident-prone robot had created the perfect distraction for the royal guards, and the three of them escaped through the door.

"We made it!" said Alfred.

However, in the corridor, something terrifying was waiting for them.

From out of the shadows it floated towards him.

The three froze.

It was the All-Seeing Eye!

CHAPTER 45

Storming of the Palace

ZAP!

ZAP!

ZAP!

Lasers shot from the centre of the flying robot's eye, and the three dodged out of the way as explosions went off all around them.

BOOM! BOOM! BOOM!

The corridor was narrow, and there was nowhere to hide.

Alfred was frozen to the spot, standing right in front of the All-Seeing Eye. None of the lasers were shooting in his direction. Why wasn't he a target? Nanny must have been telling the truth for once. They needed his blood!

The Queen grabbed her son's hand and yanked him into an alcove.

"You could have been killed," she hissed.

"It doesn't want to hurt me," he whispered back. "LOOK!"

Then Alfred stepped out into the corridor to come eye to gigantic eye with the robot again.

The Queen tried desperately to pull him down to the ground, but the boy was wilful.

"SON! NOO!" she screamed, holding on to his arm.

ZAP!

BOOM!

"ARGH!" screamed the Queen. "My eyes!"

In anger, Prince Alfred ran and leaped at the thing to make it stop. Just as he had grabbed hold of it, it whisked him up into the air at a terrific speed.

WHOOSH!

He held on for dear life as the machine flew up through the palace, leaving only Mite to tend to the Queen.

Bursting through some double doors…

BOOSH!

…the boy found himself on the ground floor of Buckingham Palace.

BOOM!

RAT-TAT-TAT!

KABOOM!

BANG! BANG! BANG!

From the sound of explosions and gunfire outside, it was clear the **revolution** was gathering pace. The **revolutionaries** must be at the palace gates already. It wouldn't be long until they would break through them and storm the palace itself.

Through yet more doors they sped, until the All-Seeing Eye stopped, with Alfred still astride it, at the palace ballroom.

There, waiting patiently for the prince, was the Lord Protector. The evil man was standing on the huge chalked pattern he'd laid out on the floor. At the centre was the statue of the griffin. All around the floor were arranged the other nine stone statues of the **King's Beasts**.

The **Lion of England.**

The **White Greyhound of Richmond.**

The Yale of Beaufort.

The RED DRAGON OF WALES.

The White Horse of Hanover.

The **White Lion of Mortimer.**

The **UNICORN OF SCOTLAND.**

The **Black Bull of Clarence.**

The Falcon of the Plantagenets.

Alfred realised that it wasn't a chessboard, after all.

It was a map.

A giant map of Britain.

Each of the ten beasts had been placed where it had come from. The dragon in Wales, the unicorn in Scotland, the lion in England, and so on.

"Your Royal Highness! How good of you to join us!" purred the Lord Protector. He did a little theatrical bow as if he were being deferential, though it was clear he was being anything but. ***"Just in time too."***

Prince Alfred slid off the All-Seeing Eye and on to his feet.

"Where is my father?" he demanded.

"I'm here, Alfred," replied the man.

Lying on the floor behind the statue of the griffin was the King. Alfred rushed over to him and fell to his knees.

"FATHER!" he cried.

The King looked like death. He was even more hollow and pale than before, and his eyes were closed.

"He has no more blood left in him," said the Lord Protector. "Which is why I need yours!"

"Son?" whispered the King, his eyes flickering open.

"Yes, Father, it's me. Alfred."

"I'm sorry, son. The Lord Protector has been controlling me for years. My mind. My body. He has weakened me to make this beast strong."

"I know, Father."

"I sent you and your mother to the Tower because I thought you would be safer there. Away from this beast."

Alfred hugged him close.

"He has been too greedy. My blood is too thin now for his wicked plan. Run, son, please run, or the Lord Protector will unleash a power so great it is impossible to imagine."

The boy rose to his feet. "No! I have to stop this evil man once and for all."

"And how, pray tell, are you going to do that, child?" purred the Lord Protector, who had been listening all along.

KABOOM!

BANG! BANG! BANG!

BOOM!

RAT-TAT-TAT!

"Can't you hear that?" exclaimed Alfred. "The revolution is underway! The people of this country have had enough of you and your evil rule. The game is over."

The Lord Protector smiled. ***"Oh no. The game has only just begun."***

He turned to the royal guards. **"SEIZE HIM!"**

At once, Prince Alfred was surrounded. Roughly, he was dragged towards the bottom of the map.

"What are you doing to me?"

"You will find out soon enough."

One of the guards passed the Lord Protector an ancient leather-bound book. Alfred could make out the gold lettering on the front. *De Libro Albion*.

"***The Book of Albion!***" exclaimed the boy.

"So you were paying attention in my Latin classes, after all," remarked the Lord Protector.

CHAPTER 46

The Book of Albion

"That one was always kept under lock and key in the palace library!" exclaimed Alfred. "I was never allowed to look at it!"

"For good reason," purred the Lord Protector. "This is the most ancient book in the world. Handwritten and illustrated by holy men centuries ago. This is the only one in existence. The only one ever made. It tells the story of the creation of Albion."

"Albion! The ancient word for Great Britain."

"Your history is not too shabby either, child. It begins with the story of the first-ever ruler of this island. Long before King Alfred. Long before official records began. Back then a beast was terrorising the people of Albion."

The Lord Protector showed the prince some of the ancient illustrations of the story. They were hand-painted and looked like the stained-glass windows you see in churches. In the pictures, there was a **huge fiery beast** with the head and wings of an eagle and the body and tail of a lion.

"A griffin!" exclaimed Alfred.

"The very same. One brave man stepped forward, and in a fearsome battle he slew the beast with this very sword."

The Lord Protector indicated the ornate sword that one of the royal guards was holding. It was the same sword with the jewelled handle he'd used to cut the palms of the King's hands and draw his blood.

The pictures in ***The Book of Albion*** showed the sword in the man's hand.

"Legend has it," continued the Lord Protector, "that once he had slain the beast, he drank its blood. Blue blood."

Indeed, in the book the griffin's blood was painted blue.

"The people of Albion fell to their knees. They believed this man now had the power of the beast. The power of life and death over all of them. Divine power ~ the power of a god."

"So that's why you need royal blood?" guessed Alfred, trying to piece together the parts of the Lord Protector's plan. "If the first-ever king of Albion, or Britain as it became known, had some of the griffin's blood mixed with his, then all of those in the royal line have a trace of the beast's blood within us."

"Exactly!" exclaimed the Lord Protector.

"That is why you needed my father's blood to bring this beast back to life."

"Yes, and why ~ now he has none left ~ I need yours."

This sent a chill down the boy's spine.

"Your evil mother, Nanny, tried to take it from me, but she failed!"

"Where is she?" asked the Lord Protector.

"Dead."

The Lord Protector paused for a moment. "She made the ultimate sacrifice for me, her son. Thank you, Mother."

Alfred shook his head. What a wicked pair. "Why is the book so important in all this?"

"*The Book of Albion* has many clues as to how this terrifying beast might one day rise again. Through the dark arts. Chants and prayers, and ancient maps. And royal blood dripping on a statue of the beast to bring it to life."

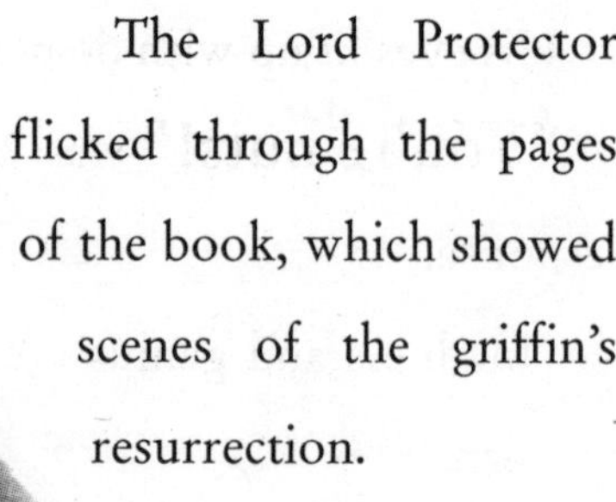

The Lord Protector flicked through the pages of the book, which showed scenes of the griffin's resurrection.

Alfred gulped…

GULP!

…and looked around the huge palace ballroom. There wasn't just the griffin. The other nine of the **King's Beasts** were placed around the map too.

"But why have you got all the statues up from the vault?" he asked.

"Because I have gone one further than ***The Book of Albion***. If I can bring the griffin back to life, why can't I bring all the **King's Beasts** to life too? With them at my side, I, and I alone, will rule this kingdom, and every other kingdom of the world, FOREVER! I will be the King of Kings for all eternity!"

His eyes lit up with demonic glee.

"You're nuts!" was Alfred's not unreasonable response.

"Madness and genius are often intertwined," said the man.

The Lord Protector turned to the guards. "Hold out the prince's hand."

Alfred struggled and struggled, and struggled some more, but it was impossible to escape their clutches. Next, the Lord Protector was handed the ancient sword. A sword that had belonged to that very first king of Albion. He held it high above his head before slicing open the palm of the boy's hand.

"ARGH!"

screamed Alfred. Next, the evil man

guided the boy closer to the statue of the griffin. His royal blood, which had left a trail on the floor, was now dripping on the eagle head of the statue.

DRIP! DRIP! DRIP!

The guards held the boy's hand in place, so more and more royal blood would drip. They began to chant, as the Lord Protector read aloud from ***The Book of Albion***.

It was Latin, and

immediately

the statue

began to

hum...

CHAPTER 47

Super-being

Gradually, the stone statue of the griffin started to glow. At first it was like there was a light burning inside, before the surface of the stone blazed like the sun. Then flames began licking the side of the statue, and the heat was so blisteringly hot it singed Alfred's pyjamas.

SIZZLE!

The Lord Protector grinned a ghoulish grin. His wicked plan was working.

Alfred noticed that the other nine statues of the **King's Beasts** had begun to hum too. **With ten beasts of fire under his control, the Lord Protector would be able to rule the world for all eternity.**

The evil man continued reading from the ancient ***Book of Albion*.**

The prince had to do something. And fast. He noticed that the royal guards either side of him had become distracted by the griffin coming to life. Now was his chance. With all his strength, Alfred pulled his arms together, so the two guards' helmets bashed.

CLONK!

Finding himself free, he surged forward towards the Lord Protector. One of the guards managed to grab the boy's arm.

"GET OFF ME!"

In the struggle, they fell hard against the glowing statue, knocking it over.

THUNK!

It toppled on to the Lord Protector.

DOOF!

The statue had become like molten lava. It burned the Lord Protector, and he convulsed on the ballroom floor in the most excruciating pain.

"AAARRRGGGHHH!"

The guards who were dotted around the room froze in fear. They didn't know what to do other than watch their evil leader writhe in agony.

"N

O

O

O!" cried the Lord Protector.

This was Alfred's moment to flee. He rushed over to the King.

"Father, Father, we have to get out of here. Now!"

The King opened his eyes. "I don't have the strength, son. You go. Flee. Flee for your life."

"Not without you!"

"Son! Look!"

The boy turned round to see the most horrifying sight.

Far from killing the Lord Protector, the statue had melted with him to create one super-being.

Made of fire, the creature was half griffin, half man.

And all

MONSTER.

It stood on two lion legs, had the talons and wings of an eagle, and the face of a man. The face of the Lord Protector.

The guards began to escape. Even the All-Seeing Eye, which presumably had seen it all, couldn't believe its eye. It was trying to fly out of harm's way. However, this monster was growing and growing as each second passed, and the palace ballroom was becoming an INFERNO!

"The sword, son, the sword!" said the King. "Help me slay the beast!"

The ancient sword was in the hands of one of the guards, who was now running away. As he dropped it on to the ballroom floor in a rush to open the door…

CLANG!

…Alfred raced over and seized it. Then he helped his father to his feet and passed him the sword. The King bravely stood right in front of the monster. It must have been at least three or four times the size of him. The King lifted the sword above his head heroically.

"I do this for Britain!" he shouted.

But, before he could strike, the griffin breathed a deadly blast of fire on him.

WHOOMPH!

It turned him to ash in a heartbeat.

All that was left of the King was a pile of **black dust.**

"NOOO!" cried Alfred.

The ancient sword fell to the floor.

CLANK!

The blade broke clean in two. Alfred snatched up the pieces, and carried them off.

Outside the ballroom windows, a group of **revolutionaries** had gathered, poised to burst into the palace itself. On seeing what had just happened, their expressions betrayed only horror. Alfred gestured for them to get back, and they hurriedly retreated.

The griffin beat its mighty wings, and began flying towards the boy, backing him into a corner. **King Alfred, as he now was with his father gone, was prepared to meet his destiny.**

PART FIVE

THE FINAL RECKONING

CHAPTER 48

Fireball

"Lionheart?" came a shout. It was his mother, the Queen, still blinded by the laser blast from the All-Seeing Eye. She had finally found her way up to the ballroom with the help of Mite, who was holding her hand tight.

Now the griffin was touching the other nine stone statues arranged on the map with its wings of fire. One by one, each of the King's Beasts was brought to life.

The statue of the lion burst into flames and roared.

Next, the UNICORN turned from stone to fire and kicked up on its hind legs.

The falcon flapped its wings of fire and squawked.

The stone white horse turned as hot as the sun.

The **yale** glowed red and gold with the heat and swivelled its horns.

The **black bull** blistered into being and began charging around the ballroom, bellowing.

The **white lion** leaped up and roared.

The giant **greyhound** growled, baring its hideous fangs.

Finally, the DRAGON OF WALES exploded into life, breathing fire from its mouth.

"Mama! No! Get back!" shouted Alfred. "**The King's Beasts!** They're all alive!"

"There is a secret way out of the ballroom!" shouted the Queen. "Mite! Pull the cord on the curtains!"

Mite did as she was told.

SHTUM!

"What's happened?" demanded the Queen.

"The curtains have closed," replied the girl, not unreasonably, as that was exactly what had happened.

"THE OTHER CORD!" cried the Queen.

Mite pulled it and to her surprise a mirror in the wall swung open.

SWING!

Alfred, Mite and the Queen all escaped through it.

The three were now in Buckingham Palace's banqueting hall. Enormous tables were placed in the shape of a U, all laid out for some grand dinner from decades ago. Broken glass and smashed crockery were everywhere, linked by cobwebs that were so huge at first glance they looked like dustsheets.

Immediately, Alfred and Mite went about barricading themselves in by pushing one of the tables up against the mirror.

SHUNT!

Then Alfred whisked one of the tablecloths off the table, and shouted to the other two, "HIDE!" All three huddled together under the long table. Rats scurried around them, looking for scraps of rotten food. It took all their willpower not to cry out as the vermin nibbled at their feet.

SQUEAK! SQUEAK! SQUEAK!

Alfred waved what was left of the sword at them.

"Shoo! Shoo! Shoo!" he said as the rats scattered.

Suddenly there was the sound of a laser blast.

ZAP!

The mirror exploded...

KABOOM!

...and shattered on the floor.

CRUNCH! CRANCH! CRINCH!

From under the table, Alfred and Mite spied the All-Seeing Eye hovering around the banqueting hall. It was searching for them. When it had just passed him, Alfred crawled out from his hiding place, and threw the tablecloth over it.

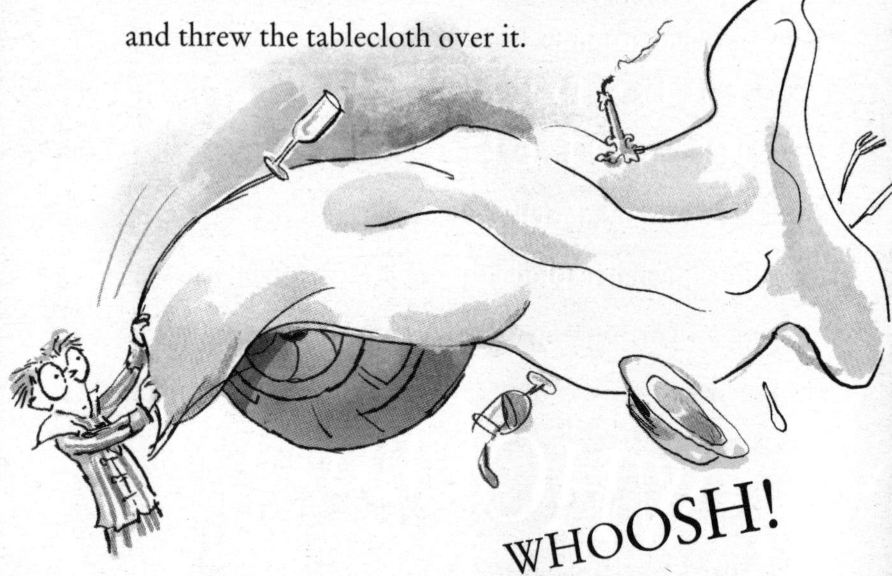

Blinded, the robot went berserk. It zoomed this way and that, desperately trying to shake off the tablecloth. It smashed into the chandeliers...

CRASH!

...scattering shards of glass everywhere. Then the All-Seeing Eye dropped to the floor.

THUD!

And rolled around.

TRUNDLE! TRUNDLE! TRUNDLE!

In an instant, the tall double doors to the banqueting hall exploded in a fireball.

WHOOMPH!

CHAPTER 49

A Final Farewell

All ten of the **King's Beasts** entered the banqueting hall in a blaze of heat and light.

The griffin with the face of the Lord Protector led the way, with the others fanned out behind.

Perhaps thinking the thing under the tablecloth was the boy, the monster breathed its deadly fire on to it.

WHOOMPH!

The robot exploded.

KABOOM!

Shards of metal shot across the banqueting hall.

TWONK! TWINK! TWUNK!

"I always hated that thing!" hissed Alfred.

As the griffin inspected the ruins of the All-Seeing Eye, Alfred whispered, "Let's get out of here!"

He stuffed the two pieces of the broken sword under his arm, and he and Mite each took one of the Queen's hands. Together the three of them scrambled as far as they could under the long tables until they reached the far side of the room. Then they bolted through the charred and smoking opening where the double doors had been.

The ten beasts tore through the tables, destroying everything in sight.

Alfred, the Queen and Mite dashed down the corridor. The two children pulled cabinets and grandfather clocks and suits of armour behind them, sending them crashing to the floor.

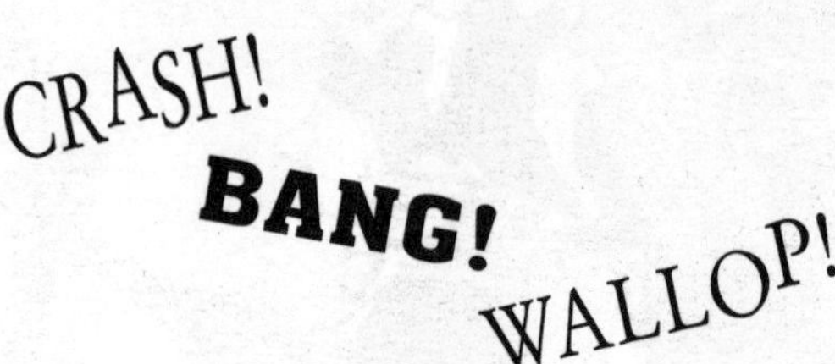

The hope was that this would slow down the beasts. However, these things had superpowers, and burned through everything in their path.

WHOOMPH! WHOOMPH! WHOOMPH!

Finally, the three had made their way to the bottom of Buckingham Palace. The vault. They hurried through the door, slamming it behind them.

There they were greeted by the sight of five of the ladies-in-waiting brandishing their weapons. The old dears had defeated every single one of the royal guards, who were all strewn across the stone floor.

"Enid?" asked Alfred.

"She didn't make it," replied Agatha sorrowfully.

"I am sorry," said the boy.

"We need to go," added Mite. "Right now."

"Why?" asked Agatha.

Just then the doors behind them burst into flames.

WHOOMPH!

The ten mighty burning beasts burst through.

SMASH!

"That's why," replied Mite. "What is the one thing that fire cannot survive?"

"Water!" answered Alfred.

"FOLLOW ME!" ordered Mite.

The unlikely band of **revolutionaries** charged across the vault. Their destination was the secret passage to the flooded **Underground** tunnel.

"Please do wait for me, your trusty robo-butler!" came a robotic voice. It was OCTOBUT, or rather Unibut, with its one lonely arm still just intact. If it had lost that one, you'd have to call it "But" and that seems plain wrong. The thing trundled after them.

The beasts gave chase, the griffin burning everything in its path.

WHOOMPH!
WHOOMPH!
WHOOMPH!

All those precious antiques (and some unwanted gifts) exploded in flames.

BOOM!

Mite found the stone in the floor of the vault, and one by one the gang raced down the stone steps and leaped into the water.

SPLISH!
SPLASH!
SPLOSH!

Alfred went last, putting the parts of the sword in his mouth like a pirate.

They swam and swam until they reached the submarine. Then they climbed down the rusty old ladder into the vessel. Alfred carried the OCTOBUT, and Agatha carried the Old Queen's box of matches.

There were just two matches left. Agatha lit the first one…

STRIKE!

…and let it burn slowly down to its very end.

"Mama," said the boy.

"Yes, Alfred?"

"Father is dead."

"No!"

Alfred hugged his blinded mother tight as they both rocked with tears.

"He loved you."

"I know. I loved him too. He died a hero, trying to slay the beast."

"I always knew, despite everything, that he was a good man."

"He truly was. He made the ultimate sacrifice for all of us. Now we have to honour him."

"You are right," replied the Queen.

"How can we defeat these monsters?" asked Mite.

"Only with this sword," replied Alfred. "The sword of the first king of Albion. And, look, it is broken in two."

"We still have one torpedo left!" chirped Agatha.

The boy's face lit up at a thought. "Maybe, just *maybe*, if we strap what is left of the sword to the torpedo, then it can deliver the fatal blow."

"Cool!" said Mite.

"Let's try," said Alfred, examining the pieces of the ancient sword.

"But the submarine is stuck in this rotten tunnel,"

said the Queen. "If we fire the torpedo from here, it will destroy all of Buckingham Palace as well."

Alfred thought for a moment. "And it will destroy us too."

"No," said the Queen. "It will destroy me."

"What?" asked Mite.

"You two are young – you can help rebuild this once-great country. If you guide my finger to the button, I can press it. Then I can be in the sky with my darling husband."

"NO!" replied Alfred. "NEVER! I won't let you do it. I am King now, and *I* will lay down my life for the people of this country."

"I will not hear of it!" said the Queen.

"Then let me do it!" pleaded Agatha.

All the surviving ladies-in-waiting were willing to lay down their lives too.

"Or me!"

"Let me!"

"Please, me!"

Apart from one.

"I would rather it wasn't me!"

"No, ladies!" replied the Queen sharply. "I won't hear of it. I always swore I would do anything for this country. And I am prepared to make the ultimate sacrifice."

All fell silent in awe of this great woman.

"I love you, Mama," said Alfred. "More than anything in the world."

"I love you too, King Alfred. More than you will ever know."

Alfred was the name of the first king of England, and this boy was determined he would not be the last.

He took the broken sword, strapped the pieces to the torpedo using some rope and tugged tight on the ends so they would stay in place.

Together the ladies-in-waiting lifted the torpedo and loaded it into the tube.

CLUNK!

Then, with great tenderness, the boy guided his mother's finger over to the **FIRE** button.

"There," he said.

CRUNCH!

The HMS *SCEPTRE* sounded as if it were breaking up in the tunnel. It lurched to one side.

TWONK!

Water began gushing in.

WHOOSH!

All those on board were swept on to the floor of the submarine.

"ARGH!"

"HELP!"

"NOO!"

"I don't think I'm going to be able to keep my

finger on the button!" panicked the Queen.

"Then I will keep you company, Your Majesty," piped up the robot butler.

"Thank you, OCTOBUT!" replied the Queen.

"I want to do something useful," it said. "Just once in my life."

"Mite, how long will it take us to swim down the tunnel out to the Thames?" asked Alfred.

"One minute," replied the girl. Then she looked towards the five ladies in their eighties and nineties. "Actually, make that five minutes."

"Mama, wait until then, then press the button."

"*I will. Give me a kiss, my beautiful boy.*"

Alfred kissed his mother on the lips. Just once. Softly and sweetly.

"Goodbye," he said.

"*Goodbye, Lionheart,*" she answered.

"Ta-ta!" chirped the OCTOBUT.

Then the Queen started to count. **"One, two, three…"**

"Let's go!" said Mite.

CRUNCH!

The submarine continued to break up.

"OCTOBUT is still holding my finger on the button!" the Queen called out. **"Four, five, six..."**

As the last match burned down, Alfred, Mite and the five ladies-in-waiting all scrambled up the ladder to the top of the submarine, and then dived into the water.

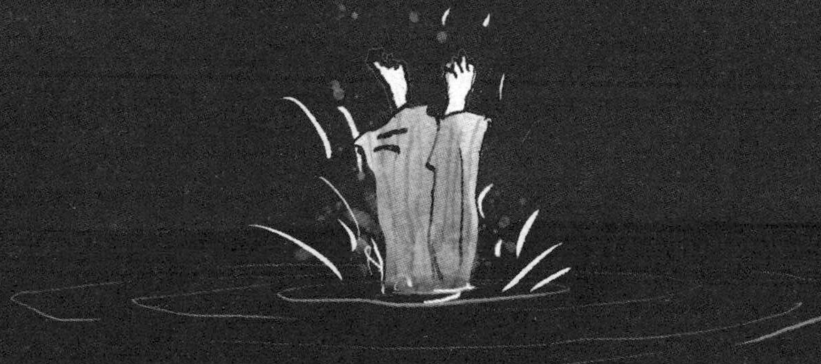

CHAPTER 50

Light

As bats attacked them from above…

SQUEAK! SQUEAK! SQUEAK!

…the gang swam for their lives. When the two children and the old ladies had reached the end of the Underground tunnel, they dived down through the underwater passage that led out to the Thames.

GASP!

As soon as they came up for air, they could see something terrifying in the distance. Buckingham Palace was illuminated by red and gold light. The ten flaming **King's Beasts**, led by the griffin, were emerging from the top of the palace, and letting off their deafening cries.

The dragon was breathing fire at those on the ground.

WHOOMPH!

The poor people were fleeing for their lives as the earth was scorched around them.

The Lord Protector's airship descended through the clouds and began blasting the **revolutionaries** as they fled.

ZAP! ZAP! ZAP!

BOOM! BOOM! BOOM!

"Mama! Now!" cried Alfred, even though she couldn't hear him. "NOW!"

Just then there was an almighty blast.

KABOOM!

Buckingham Palace, the home of the royal family for hundreds of years, exploded.

Shards of the ancient sword glistened magically as they tore into the beasts.

They let out blood-curdling cries.

"AAAAARRRRRGGGGGHHHHH!"

The fire caught the airship, and it burst into flames.

BOOM!

It plunged to the ground.

CRASH!

Thick black smoke billowed up into the sky.

WHOOSH!

For a moment, the shapes of the beasts could be seen within the black clouds. The griffin beat its mighty wings one last time as the Lord Protector's face let out a silent scream. Then all ten of the **King's Beasts** vanished into air.

Into

thin

air.

Mite hauled herself out of the Thames and on to the riverbank, before giving a helping hand to the five elderly ladies and the young King.

Thousands of people were now swarming all over the city, watching the clouds of smoke from Buckingham Palace snake up into the sky.

A sky where now the Queen had joined her King.

The people were dirty and dressed in rags. The young King, his face blackened, and his ripped pyjamas wet through from the river, fitted in perfectly with them. As Alfred had been kept under lock and key in Buckingham Palace for his entire life, none of the people recognised him.

"Your Majesty," began Agatha.

"Shush," shushed the young King. "Alfred is fine."

"Aren't you going to tell them all who you are?"

"Why should I?" asked Alfred.

"Because we need to rebuild this kingdom," reasoned Agatha.

"Yes. And we all need to do it together. Everyone equal, and as one."

"Cool!" remarked Mite.

"Come on…"

The ladies-in-waiting began tending to the sick

and wounded, of which there were many. Meanwhile, Alfred took Mite's hand, and together they clambered over the rubble that was London. They headed towards what was left of Buckingham Palace. Amongst the burning rubble of the palace, Alfred found the remains of one of the **revolutionaries'** Union Jacks. The flag was blackened and burned, but still a powerful symbol of a once-great nation.

With pride, he held the flag aloft, and waved it in the air.

SWOOSH! SWOOSH!

The people stopped and listened to what this twelve-year-old boy had to say.

"This great nation belongs to us all!" he began. "Every single one of us. Every man, every woman and every child. Together, and only together, can we rebuild her. Brick by brick!"

"HOORAY!" cheered the crowd.

At that moment,

the dark clouds parted,

and the sun shone on the lonely island

for the first time in years.

"What is that?" asked Mite,

squinting up at the sky.

"Light," said the boy with a smile.

"At last. Light."

The End